To Mom, love is eternal.

PREFACE

Dolls crack and shatter
Breaking a new mold like Prometheus
Alive and sparking joy
But what happens to those who don't deserve joy?

1

LOURDE

It was after two in the morning, but I wasn't tired.

Barrett just declared he wanted to be with me.

Me.

When I asked him about the consequences of dating his best friend's younger sister, he'd said the most romantic yet disturbing thing, *"I don't give a fuck about anyone else but you. They can all perish under a cinder of smoke and ash."*

Then he proceeded to kiss me, and that's when my heart rocketed to the moon, taking off and levitating in a suspended euphoria—until we were rudely interrupted.

The untimely visit from Detective Summer and Detective Davies had kept our hands from clawing at one another. Their late-night interruption informed Barrett of a fire that had broken out on the third floor at his award-winning tower, *21 Park*, the same tower he had just sold but had yet to hand over. In the last hour, the detectives ran through what they knew so far—which wasn't much—and inquired if Barrett had any known enemies as early evidence pointed to arson.

Leaving Barrett to see the detectives out, I pushed aside

my blue evening dress and unpinned my chignon, letting my loose waves fall around my face. As I thought about this evening, a knowing smile crept onto my lips. Just a few hours earlier and consumed by jealousy, Barrett had me pinned in the dark library, his fingers inside me while my date for the evening and his family were in the dining room nearby.

But my family, and especially my brother, Conner, had no idea the man I was most interested in was Barrett Black. The same man who only days earlier in the Hamptons had rejected me when I'd told him he'd stolen my heart. My opinion on my love life didn't matter to Mom, all she cared about was finding me a husband from a noteworthy family, so I could be married off and follow in her footsteps.

Enter Exhibit A, Finigan Connolly, son of James Connolly, the Governor of Massachusetts, and the family of politicians stemming back to the 1900s. Old money, not nouveau riche. A perfect match in Mom's eyes.

Sure, Finigan was cute—in a Zac Efron kind of way—but he wasn't Barrett.

No one could ever be Barrett Black.

Dark green eyes, mysterious and bone-meltingly sexy, Barrett was the guy whose scorching good looks and mysterious glances kept me intrigued. Once a silly crush, held over many years, transformed into something bigger when he let me into his Hamptons home, after yet another failed relationship. The forbidden attraction we had was reserved only for one another. Difficult to control our urges in such proximity, his touches and stares all culminated in a secret and forbidden attraction, and the crush I had on Connor's best friend turned into a full-blown love affair.

The ding of the elevator interrupted my dirty thoughts. I looked up to see Barrett staring at me, and the detectives gone, presumably headed back down to the Manhattan sidewalk.

"Right, where were we?" he asked. Dressed in charcoal suit pants molded to his thighs and a crisp white shirt, he stood with a hint of a smile. His green eyes like magnets, dragging me toward him, I shrugged, my teeth grazing across my bottom lip.

Each step he took closer, my heart pounded harder against my chest, knocking the breath from my lungs.

"You're coming with me." He bent down and pulled me into his arms.

"Wait!"

"I've waited long enough having the two detectives here while imagining my head between your thighs tasting you." His eyes darkened as his heated gaze fell to my lips. "Now I have you, Lourde. I want to claim you, every last inch."

Oh.

I swallowed. Without any hesitation, I pulled myself closer into his chest, wrapping my arms around his broad shoulders.

Strong arms carried me, clutching me tightly against his muscular wall with each step he took. I nuzzled into his neck, his manly scent making my lady parts squeeze together in anticipation. He kicked open a door leading into his bedroom, staring at my exposed thigh, where the slit of my dress had opened wide.

After years of crushing hard on Barrett Black and imagining him taking me in his bedroom, I was finally here in his arms. I took it all in, unsure of what I expected to find. His low-line enormous bed took center stage in his room across the expansive cement floors. Above it, vaulted ceilings with exposed black metal beams held a chandelier overhead as alabaster walls stood bare like an empty art gallery.

"Going for minimal?" I asked.

"Haven't had time to decorate." Without another word, he slammed his lips to mine in a heated kiss infused with desire.

I pulled away, breathless and slightly confused. "But haven't you been here for years?"

"I think I need to hush that pretty mouth." His mouth lowered to mine as his tongue traced the curve of my bottom lip before he bit down on it just enough to elicit pain and pleasure, then tossed me onto the middle of his bed.

"Ow." I reached for my lip and gazed up at him. He'd already removed his shirt and cast it to the floor. His forged and rippling muscles had me forgetting about my momentary tingling lip and lusting after every curve of his torso. I watched as Barrett slipped out of his pants. His thick erection sprung free and a warmth pooled between my legs. Carved from granite, the man was all mine.

As I dragged my gaze up, I spread my legs apart. Hungry eyes stared back at me when my eyes met his. Then his heated stare fell on my breasts, hovering there before he lowered it to the opening of my dress.

His almond-shaped jade eyes were enough to set me on fire. He bent down and climbed on the bed and between my legs, his hands on either side of my head where he rested his weight. Lowering his mouth to mine, he said, "What do you want, dollface?"

I breathed him in, my heart slamming against my chest. Fuck, I could bottle his scent— delicious, sharp, mysterious—an orgasm in a bottle. "I want you, Barrett. It's always been you."

Barrett pressed his lips to mine, and our tongues

collided in a feverish assault on one another. His fingers slid underneath the strap of my dress, pushing one down, then the next, my nipples hardening as they brushed against his hard chest.

His erection dug between my thighs as I widened more for him. Clenching my sex, I grabbed his ass and pulled him down at the same time, raising my hips to feel him against my clit.

"You like my cock there?" He pressed down harder on my clit while tracing my neck down to the shell of my breasts with his mouth. His dirty words combined with his touch had me teetering on the edge. *Fuck*, he wasn't even inside me.

I moaned out. Barrett took one breast into his mouth and sucked hard on my nipple, dragging his teeth around it. His hand slid up the inside of my thigh and pushed across my lace thong, then he plunged two fingers inside me, dragging my wetness to my nub.

Yes. Fuck, yes.

His fingers returned and curved inside of me, my eyes shut tight. A shot of warmth tingled through my lower belly, and seconds later, I screamed his name out in a moan.

Opening my eyes, I found his fiery gaze staring back at me. He took his fingers to his mouth and licked my wetness off of them, one at a time, while never breaking eye contact.

"I want you to taste how delicious you are, Lourde."

Oh my.

With my pussy still throbbing, he brushed his glistening finger to my lips, and I took it in my mouth. Tasting my own juices on his finger, I closed my eyes while imagining I was giving him glorious head.

"Fuck," he groaned, removing his finger. He then

leaned in, dragging his lips across mine in a savage kiss. Our teeth clashed, his tongue pressed against mine as my fingers felt for his hair, tugging at the roots while he deepened the kiss, assaulting all my senses.

I removed my mouth from his, breathless and needy, the ache between my thighs almost becoming unbearable.

"Ride me, dollface," he ordered. "I want to see your delicious tits up in my face."

I groaned out in obedience, his dirty words had my lady bits singing "Hallelujah." Sitting up, I unzipped the dress, flinging it to the floor, then lowered the scrap of material acting as a thong.

He opened his side drawer and reached for the foil packet. Taking it to his teeth, he tore it open and wrapped himself. Then, lying back and folding his arms behind his head, he watched me like a predator stalking their prey.

"Leave the stilettos on." With his voice like gravel and hooded eyes, goosebumps erupted all over my skin.

"Deal."

With my four-inch heels snaking around my ankles, I climbed on top of him.

My fingers gripped firmly around his cock, and I lowered myself onto him. A deep, guttural moan sounded from the back of his throat as I slowly glided down onto him. Absorbing his thickness inside me, I grabbed my breast and squeezed, savoring the aching pain brewing inside me.

"Fuck, you're too much to take like this, Lourde."

Folding up, his face was only inches from mine, his breath on my cheek. He fisted my hair between his fingers, tilting my head back so my tits pushed against his chest. He took his mouth to mine, raking his tongue across my bottom teeth. I leveled down on him deeper, sliding back and forth.

"Tell me it's only me, Lourde."

He sunk his teeth across my neck, his warm breath sending pulses between my legs.

"Just you." I breathed out, my body hot, aching all over with a compulsion for him.

He cupped my ass, squeezing it tight, pushing me into him harder and faster.

His finger teased my back entrance, and every nerve ending burst alive. I moaned out his name as my body became dead-heavy.

"Fuck, Lourde," he hissed out, his head dropping, his breath on my shoulder.

We stayed like this, neither one of us wanting to move as our chests rose and fell, slowly returning to any semblance of normality.

2

BARRETT

She'd spent the entire weekend at my apartment in the Upper West Side, and I didn't want her to leave. We'd lived between the sheets most of the time, only leaving for food and water. But on the short ride from my apartment to her parents' house on Park Avenue, she was mouse quiet.

Maybe I made a mistake. I asked Lourde to move in with me this morning over breakfast, and she declined, saying one step at a time.

Had I freaked her out with the whole move-in question? Was it so weird to think she'd want to actually move in with me? I shook my head. Jesus, fuck, what was I thinking? She was right. We hadn't even told Connor yet.

I pulled up to the front of the house and killed the engine of my McLaren GT.

"The weekend was magical," she said in a soft whisper I'd only just heard.

"It was. Thanks for taking a chance on me, Lourde. I'm not perfect, but I know everything makes sense with you in my life."

"I miss you already." Leaning in, she planted her lips on mine in a kiss that I didn't want to end. My hand wrapped around the nape of her neck, squeezing her closer. She groaned in my mouth, and my dick responded, swelling in the seam of my pants.

She pulled away and smirked, her pupils dilated. A dark and wanting need filled me as it did her.

"Don't go," I said, clearing my sandpaper voice.

"I have to. We don't want anyone asking questions."

"Fuck their questions," I said, wanting to taste her again. I wanted to wake to her soft breath on my pillow, the rise and fall of her chest on mine. "Meet me for lunch tomorrow?"

She smiled and something stirred inside of my chest.

"Okay."

"My office at one?"

"But people will know."

"All they know is that you're Lourde Diamond, Connor's sister, who they know is my friend."

She mulled it over for way too long, and each second that ticked by, the hammering in my chest grew louder. *What the fuck was that?*

"I'll see you there."

And with that, I planted another kiss on her swollen lips. Suddenly, she pulled away a blush dusted her cheeks.

"I should go."

"You should go," I echoed.

And she exited the car with an impossibly beautiful grin on her creamy and blushed complexion.

* * *

I checked the gunmetal gray clock face of my Cartier watch. It was nearing one o'clock. Lourde would be here any moment, so wrapping this meeting up with the department heads was a priority. It had been a clusterfuck of a morning with detectives and a brewing media storm out front of the building, but I didn't care. I was riding on the high-tide that was Lourde.

"Olivia, do we know why Jessica resigned without notice?"

"No idea. I tried calling her, but she hasn't returned any of my phone calls."

"That's odd. Can anyone shed any light on why she may have quit so suddenly?"

I looked around at the four other faces looking hungover as fuck.

"No idea," Tobias, my logistical manager, said.

"Same here, although I saw her come out of the women's bathrooms last week with tears in her eyes," Sam, my head of construction, volunteered.

I looked over at Ivy, my media director. Maybe she knew what was going on. After all, she knew most things around here. "No idea, I barely knew her."

Great.

"She was managing the interior decorating installation in the townhouses in Brooklyn. Now, I have all of that on top of what's already on my plate," Olivia said.

"Can you still finish it on time?"

"I don't know." Olivia shook her head, and I knew she was being brutally honest. Olivia was one of my hardest-working and loyal employees, but even she had her limits.

"It has to be. I have the new owners moving in two weeks." Tobias let out a huff.

Something pulled my attention from my team and to my left, past the glass-framed boardroom toward the reception desk.

Dressed in a cinched violet dress offset by her silky

cream skin and brown shoulder-length hair, Lourde stole the breath from my lungs.

"Thanks, everyone," I said, casting my eyes back to the table. "We'll work it out, Olivia."

Ivy stood, gathering her laptop. "Barrett, we still need to address the media about the fire at 21 Park."

"There's nothing to say until we hear more from the engineers."

She mumbled something inaudible.

"Just draft something for me to look at," I said.

"Do they suspect arson?" Olivia asked.

"It appears so. The detectives aren't giving too much away, as usual," I added. Vivid memories of the detectives hovering over my dead mother flooded into view, and I pushed them away as soon as they surfaced. Having them at the house brought all that up again, but with Lourde by my side, my discomfort melted away.

Olivia side-eyed me, fumbling with her folders. If I didn't know any better, she wanted to talk to me without the prying ears of her colleagues.

After Ivy, Tobias, and Sam walked out the door, she lifted her head. *Knew it.*

"Is that Lourde Diamond in reception?"

I glanced over to reception like I hadn't noticed her as soon as she walked in. "I guess it is."

"What is *she* doing here?" She popped up an accusatory, heavily plucked eyebrow.

"We're friends."

"You don't have any female friends."

It was my turn to raise an eyebrow. "Olivia, I think you have loads to do, don't you?"

"Maybe she wants a job. I'm sure she'd know about prestige interiors," she muttered while collecting the last of her things.

"Maybe that's not a bad idea."

"You're serious?" Olivia stared at me while I mulled it over.

She'd been wanting to work but couldn't because her parents wouldn't let her—Diamond women never worked. Literally up until last week when her father, Alfred, changed his mind, she hadn't worked a day in her life. Maybe this could be the opportunity she might be after. The timing couldn't have been better.

"Absolutely. Who do we know who can cover you on short notice? She's a friend. I'm sure she'd love to help."

"Well, that would be amazing. I'm already working sixteen-hour days as it is, and with Jessica throwing in the towel, I'm up to my ears in work with the handover of the Brooklyn townhouses."

"Well, I can only ask," I said, not promising anything. Lourde probably wouldn't even consider it, but it was worth a try.

"Who can say no to Barrett Black?"

"You, all the damn time, Olivia."

"You pay me to say no! Anyway, you're like a brother to me. Someone has to withstand the charming effects you have on women." She put her fingers in her mouth like she was going to gag.

I chuckled out a laugh and stood, not wanting to leave Lourde waiting any longer. As I walked toward the foyer, Lourde sat admiring the three-dimensional miniature building of 21 Park, the tower my company, ZF Construction, recently sold to a Russian billionaire. She stood up when she saw me and smoothed down her dress. I felt the weight of the stare from the woman behind the reception desk.

There was something so real and hot about Lourde standing in my foyer—I wanted to take her here and now.

"Lourde, so nice to see you." I turned to find four sets of women's eyes were on me.

"Thanks for seeing me on such short notice, Barrett," she said, playing along.

"Follow me," I said, turning and leading her out of the foyer.

"Everyone is staring at me," she said, her voice low as she took in the open-plan offices.

"Because you're beautiful." I felt her turn toward me, and a grin lifted on my mouth.

"And so is everyone else here."

Damn. Okay, so once upon a time, I may have only hired women I found attractive. But, in my defense, all the shitty ones were fired, and the remaining staff did have actual skills.

My assistant, Aimee, was mid-call when Lourde and I walked by, her expression fucking priceless.

"Here we are," I said, pushing open the doors to my corner office and letting her walk ahead of me.

I shut the door behind us, not before peering beyond the open space to my staff who dared to look my way.

"Wow, Barrett, this is something," she said, walking toward the view from the thirty-third floor. It was a pretty spectacular view, one I rarely had time to take in.

As I approached Lourde, her vanilla-blossom scent and freshly washed hair surrounded me, and as I stopped just behind her, it invaded my senses completely, making me forget about the never-ending work pressures that awaited me.

"So now that you have me here. What is it you want to do with me?"

"Oh, there are many things, dollface." My voice was

gravelly low. "My walnut desk, I imagine you spread-eagled as I ground you out with my tongue."

"Is that so, Mr. Black?" she hummed, still staring out the window, my body pressed against hers.

"Then I'd spin you around and fuck you hard up against the polished edge with my hand across your throat so you couldn't make a sound."

She turned around, her cheeks burnished bright pink, her chest rising and falling.

"I think I'd like that," she said breathlessly, and my dick came to attention in my suit pants.

"Would you now?"

She nodded. The innocent Lourde Diamond wanted this as much as I did. Her wish was my fucking command. I walked to the front of my desk and pressed the button to my executive assistant.

"Yes, Mr. Black."

"Hold all my calls, Aimee. I don't want to be interrupted."

"Yes, sir."

I hung up, walked over to the door, and quietly clicked the lock.

She had already made her way over to my desk, her peach of an ass on the edge as I walked toward her.

Stopping in front of her, I crossed my arms over my chest. "Pull your dress above your thighs."

She reached below the hem with her two fingers and pulled it up and above her thighs, revealing a pink lace thong.

I adjusted myself, uncomfortable from my swelling dick pressing against the zipper of my suit pants.

"Now take off your thong but leave your stilettos on."

She did as I asked, and spellbound by her beauty, I watched on greedily taking in all of her.

"Lie back on the desk and spread your legs wide for me, dollface. I want to see all of you."

She blinked but did exactly that. Fuck, her delicious cunt was there for the taking, and I couldn't wait any longer. Kneeling, I dragged her forward, placing her thighs on my shoulders, and my tongue plowed into her folds, lapping up all of her.

A groan escaped her lips but only loud enough for me to hear. I was just as eager as she was, and I plunged into her again. Wet and sweet, my tongue lavished her over and over, dragging her wetness up to her clit.

"Barrett," she breathed.

"I need to be inside you, dollface.

"Yes," she whispered. "Now."

I got up off my knees and stalked round to the drawers of my desk. Opening the bottom drawer, I pulled out a foil packet feeling her gaze on me.

"In case of emergencies?" she asked. "I can see why, looking around here at all the models you have working for you."

Was she seriously jealous right now?

Walking back around to her, I possessively pushed my body against hers, wrapping my hands around her waist, the force moving the desk back. Seething mad, I couldn't believe she thought there could be anyone else but her.

"There's only you, Lourde." I unzipped my pants and rolled on the condom.

"Is there?" she asked, taking her teeth across her bottom lip.

"You know there is. You're all I fucking think about."

"Show me," she said, taking her lips to mine in a rough, heated, and possessive kiss.

"Do you like to make me mad so I fuck you harder, dollface?"

Embarrassed, she looked away.

I pinched her chin between my fingers, tilting her head so she faced me.

"Maybe." She shrugged, and fire flowed through my veins.

"Turn around," I said, my voice coming out in a harsh whisper.

As soon as she faced the desk, I plunged into her, and she let out an audible gasp. "Quiet," I said, my mouth to her ear.

I wrapped my hand around the column of her neck. "Is this what you want?"

She nodded, and I squeezed tighter. I fucked her harder while I maintained the gentle pressure to her neck.

"Make me mad again, and I'll assault your asshole," I warned, pulling out and rubbing my tip against her puckered entrance before sinking back into her pussy.

She moaned and writhed around me, finding her release as she clamped down on my cock.

Fuck me, she was up for anything. I was done for. Heat slashed my chest, and with a few more thrusts, I spilled all I had into her, dropping my hand and holding her waist as I hugged her from behind.

We stayed like this for a moment while we caught our breaths, then I slid out of her and headed toward my private bathroom to clean myself up.

When I walked back in, she had smoothed down her dress and was raking her fingers through her hair, combing it to an orderly display.

"That was…" she shook her head. "I want that every day."

I laughed. "Maybe if you worked for me, I'd make that a reality, dollface."

She stopped threading her fingers through her hair.

"What?"

"Olivia, my interior designer, noticed you in the foyer, and it was all her idea. But it makes sense. Hear me out. You've grown up around luxury. You know what looks good and what doesn't."

She shrugged. "Sure."

"I have eight townhouses that need managing for the sale in two weeks, and my second-in- charge, Jessica, has just quit without notice. They have designed everything. It's just about pulling it all together."

"But I don't have any hands-on experience. You know this. I've never worked in my twenty-three trips around the sun!"

"So what do you have to lose? Try it. It's only for two weeks, and it's in Brooklyn."

"Guess it sounds fun." Her grin was quickly replaced with fear. "What if I fuck it up for you?"

"You won't."

She thrust a hand on her hip. "I'm glad you're confident! What about us then?"

"What about us?"

"Do you think we can keep this a secret with me around here?"

"I can if you can."

She twisted her lips into a smile. "It sounds perfect except for one thing."

"What?"

"My brother, what the hell would he say?"

"I forgot about Connor." I folded my arms. "Let's just say we became good friends in the Hamptons."

She twisted her lips. "That could work, and he knows I've always been interested in design."

"See, I didn't even know that about you. Maybe after these two weeks, if you like it, you can stay on."

"Maybe. So does that make you my boss?" Her hazel eyes were wide and round.

"Your boss' boss."

"I see."

"So you in?"

"I'm in," she said with a wide grin.

I kissed her while pulling her into my chest, my insides vibrating with happiness.

"You won't get bored seeing me every day?" Her brows pinched together.

Was she serious?

"I told you, it's only you, Lourde." I squeezed her around the waist, my lips invading hers with a tender kiss.

I abruptly pulled away, breathless. "Lunch. If we don't go now, I'll want to taste you again."

She giggled as she placed her hand in mine.

"Good, because not only are we celebrating my new job, but I'm going to tell Mom and Dad I'm moving out tonight at dinner."

"You are?" I exclaimed.

"Into my own apartment."

Someone just got a pin and burst my balloon. My face crestfallen, my lungs deflated as the news of her moving out hit me between the ribs.

"No one knows about us, Barrett. We can't move in yet… baby steps, okay?"

"I fucking hate baby steps."

"I know." She held her hand to my cheek but didn't offer anything further.

All I wanted to do was wake up next to her each morning and show the world she was mine. And it was starting to bother me she didn't want to go public with our relationship.

Why didn't she?

3

LOURDE

Everything in the world was right. Mind-blowing sex with Barrett on his walnut desk while he gently squeezed my neck. *Oh hell, I need more of that.* A new job and now the only thing holding me back from true and utter liberation was minutes away.

Mom and Dad sat at opposite ends of the dinner table with me between them. They hadn't said much to each other all evening, and this was becoming the new normal.

I twirled the last strand of pasta on my fork and swallowed it down while checking my phone. My two besties, Pepper and Grace, were still in the Hamptons with their boyfriends. I'd been slack, not getting back to their mountains of texts and calls. The last time we spoke, I was crying my eyes out on the ride back from the Hamptons when Barrett didn't want anything to do with me, and now, well, we had so much to talk about.

I put my iPhone down, resolute on calling them back tonight. I'd finished my plate of tagliatelle vongole, and it was now or never.

Telling them about my new job could wait. I had more important things on my mind. I took a deep breath to try to figure out how to approach them with the news.

Screw it, no time like the present.

"So, Mom, Dad, I'm moving out."

There it is.

The clang of Mom's cutlery pulled everyone's attention.

"What? Why?" She gasped, taking her hand to her head and patting her forehead in distress over my announcement.

"Because I'm twenty-three, Mom, and I need my space."

"Where are you thinking, luv?" Dad asked, taking the napkin to his mouth.

"I don't know. I was hoping I could stay in one of your apartments, maybe in Tribeca or Soho?"

"Of course, dear, you can stay in any of them," Dad said.

"But Alfred, shouldn't we discuss this?" Mom glared at her husband.

"I don't see why. Lourde is a responsible adult who can choose her own path in life."

The way he rounded out *choose* had me wondering if he felt stifled and trapped like me. But everything was all right between my parents, *wasn't it?* They seemed to argue more lately, and I wondered if it was to do with the stress of Dad stepping down soon and grooming my brother to take over the media empire—which it seemed he wasn't really interested in—or was it something else?

Dad stood, his fingers splayed across the marble table as he rested on it. "I think you should do it, although this house will definitely miss your presence. You do you, Lourde."

"Thanks, Daddy." Instantly I got up, my movement sending the chair dragging back on the marble tiles. I walked over and stepped in to hug him, squeezing him tight.

Mom huffed out a sigh. "If that's what you truly want, Lourde, then I think the Tribeca apartment would be perfect. It has more security than any of the others."

Not believing that this day could get any better, I moved away from Dad and toward Mom. "Mom, thank you," I said, giving her an awkward, half-standing, half-sitting hug.

"You want a job and now you're moving out!" She shook her head. "What's next?"

Unsure if her question was rhetorical or not, I stayed silent.

"You're right, this place will be so empty without you in it, Lourde." I saw the glare she threw at her husband, but I didn't care. Right now, I had to plan moving out, and no lover's quarrel could temper my excitement.

"I've got to tell the girls!" I said, grabbing my phone and running toward my room.

I flopped down on my bed and kicked my legs back and forth, unable to contain my excitement.

Quickly, I video dialed Pepper and Grace.

"What's up, girlfriend" Pepper smiled, her lips cherry red and unruly black curls surrounding her face.

"Pepper!" I shrieked. "I'm moving out."

"You're what?" Grace said, joining the call.

"I am moving out. I told Mom and Dad tonight at dinner, and they gave me their blessing."

"Finally!" Pepper clapped her hands together. "Where to?"

"Their apartment in Tribeca. Apparently, it has extra security, and it's in a really cool part of town. I'm just so excited. Will you come back and help me move in?" I pleaded.

"Absolutely, I could do a few days apart from Jake," Pepper said.

"Why, what's happening with Jake?" I asked.

"He's on his period. Seriously, the guy is so moody lately, he keeps calling me spoiled. Can you believe that? You know it's not my fault I come from money."

"Tell me about it." I groaned. "Hunter was the same."

Behind Pepper, I could make out my ex, Hunter, talking with Jake and Dane. It was hard to believe that only a few weeks earlier, I was in the Hamptons with my now ex, Hunter, thinking he was going to propose but instead, finding him fucking some bimbo in the sand dunes.

With nowhere to go, my brother called his best friend, Barrett Black, knowing he was in the Hamptons for work. Barrett picked me up, took me in, and that's when my brother's best friend turned into way more than I expected, even though I always wanted it to. He opened my eyes to possibilities beyond the chains of my rich and glamorous existence.

"These guys just throw that in our face. Sometimes Dane makes comments. I just have to brush off," Grace said.

"Anyway, screw him. It's not about Jake and me. It is about you."

"How have you been since the Barrett breakup? You were so distraught on the drive back, but it's like you've forgotten about him!" Grace said.

"It's probably because of Finigan Connolly," Pepper added.

"Oh." I paused. "Yeah, a lot has happened since then."

"Since Thursday? Today's Monday!" Pepper said.

"How was dinner with Finigan? Do you like him? He's cute, right?" Grace's questions came out in rapid fire.

"Finigan's cute, but well, Barrett came to dinner and then cornered me before he left and asked me to go to his house after."

"Wait. Why did Barrett come to dinner? Wasn't he here in the Hamptons? Oh my God, how awkward!" Pepper laughed.

"You could say that."

"Barrett had to watch you with Finigan? That would have been torture." Grace pursed her lips at the thought.

"I didn't make it easy on him, either. I was flirty and touchy with Finigan."

They both split into strained laughter.

"You're blushing, Lourde. Tell us what happened? Are you back together?" Pepper asked.

"Oh, I hope so!" Grace's voice was noticeably high-pitched. These girls knew how much I crushed hard on Barrett for years. They were just as part of this romance as I was. Okay, well, almost.

"Make sure no one, and I mean no one, can hear this!" I pleaded with a stern voice.

Pepper glanced over her shoulder. "I couldn't give a fuck what Jake thinks right now. He's probably ogling some little social climber over the balcony with your ex."

"Okay, chill, negative Nancy," Grace said.

"I went to his place like he asked only to thank him."

"What for?"

"Because my parents allowed me to get a job because of what he said."

"Wait, hang on. It's only been a few days, and you're telling me you're getting a job, you're back with Barrett, and you're moving out?" Grace asked.

I squealed. "Uh-huh."

"Shhh! I want to hear about Barrett!" Pepper nudged Grace.

"Okay, so I went to thank him for what he said to my dad, and then he didn't want to let me go. He said that he couldn't be without me and can't stop thinking of me." I sighed, my hands finding the ends of my hair. "That's when some detectives came and ruined our moment. and when they left, it was magical."

"Magical how?" Grace asked, her eyes like dinner plates.

I laid down on my stomach, braced on my elbows. "We made love, and he gave me three orgasms." I kicked my feet back and forth. "Is it weird that I'm imagining a wedding with him?"

"Holy shit, Lourde, what the fuck! I'm so excited, I am screaming over here." Grace jumped up, and Pepper pulled her back down.

"Yes, but it's a secret. We can't tell my family until we figure out what to say. Especially now, since I'll be working with him."

"You're working for Barrett at his construction company?" Pepper questioned.

"Only for two weeks. He just needed some help because someone quit, and apparently, I know style and design."

"Girlfriend, you know style like I know every rerun of *Sex and the City*. You were born for this job," Grace said.

"I actually think it'll be a bit of fun, but you should see all the women who work for him. I visited him today at lunch, and they're all gorgeous enough to be models. I'm sure he's slept with most of them."

"What does that matter, what he did in the past? He's

with you now. He told you he only wants to be with you," Grace said.

"I know, you're right. Still, after everything that's happened with Hunter cheating and basically every other boyfriend I've had doing the same... you have to wonder. I mean, he is one of the biggest playboys in Manhattan. He doesn't just get that title."

"And you're Lourde Diamond, heiress to a publishing empire, all-around, superhuman being and one of the most grounded women I know, and I think he knows that," Pepper said.

"Hang on, men bashers. Just because he has pretty women working for him doesn't make him a bad person. Can you guys just chill out and actually realize he's declared that he wants to be with you, Lourde? Put aside the bullshit and enjoy the ass-splitting orgasms you're getting!" Grace added, and we burst out laughing.

"Okay, maybe you're right. It's just been so amazing these last couple of days. It's almost too good to be true."

"So what is Connor saying about you working for Barrett?" Pepper asked, twisting the ends of her curly black hair.

"We haven't told him. No one knows yet. He only asked me at lunch today to work for him. I think maybe we can keep it a secret." Placing my hands on the side of my temples, I rubbed them in a circular motion. "Or do you think I should tell Connor? I could say we became great friends when I stayed at his home in the Hamptons, and I'm just helping him out as a consultant on this?"

"That could work." Grace nodded in agreement.

"I don't know. I think Connor can smell bullshit. And I think he'd be pretty hurt if he found out you were lying to him," Pepper added.

"How do you know?" I asked.

She shrugged. "I don't. It's just a hunch."

"I don't like lying about our relationship, but I think with Connor stressed at work and some discord between my parents... it's just not the right time."

"The longer you leave it, the worse it's going to get," Pepper interjected.

"You're right. Barrett wants to tell Connor. Can you believe that?" I said, half laughing.

"I can. He wants to tell the world you're his. Starting with the person who could take it the worst," Grace said.

I shook my head, dreading telling Connor. "Don't say that."

"You're going out with your brother's best friend, who, might I add, is a whole eight years older than you. Do you really think Connor is going to be cool with that?" Pepper asked.

"Maybe?"

"Get your head out of the orgasm clouds, girlfriend. He will be livid," Grace said.

"I love him," I blurted out, and it was the truth. I'd never felt like I feel now. My lungs are exploding with air and the sense of calm I feel around him is something I've never experienced before in my life."

"Oh, Lourde," Grace said." That is so sweet. Do you think he loves you?"

"Well, we haven't said it, but I think maybe?"

"Barrett Black in a relationship. Well, I thought I'd never see the day," Pepper commented.

"We're happy. I just don't want to mess it up yet by telling the world. I want us to enjoy our bubble."

"Your little love bubble." Grace smiled.

"Yes, exactly."

Grace looked over her shoulder. "Dane's calling me. I have to go."

"Will you guys pop back for my housewarming party, I'm thinking, Saturday?"

"Absolutely!" Grace squealed and pulled Pepper in tight.

"Hell, yes," Pepper added.

"Okay, I'll text you."

4

BARRETT

L
ast night, I couldn't help feeling like she rejected me, but she was so ecstatic about moving out, I didn't question it. She didn't want to tell Connor about us with whatever he had going on at work—that I understood—but still, was there some part of her resisting us?

The drone of the buzzer cut through my spiraling thoughts.

"I have Lourde Diamond here to see you."

"Thanks, Aimee, send her in, and can you ask Olivia to join us in five minutes?"

"Yes, Mr. Black."

Aimee pushed open the door, and Lourde walked through. With a soft click, Aimee closed it behind her, leaving us.

"Don't you look gorgeous on your first day of work. I don't know how I'm going to get any work done with your ass begging me to slap it in that tight skirt."

"Barrett!' she shrieked. "Well, for starters, I won't be here. I'll be in Brooklyn, remember?"

"You'll be here if I want you here," I said, dragging my gaze across the open neck of her silk blouse.

She pulled an imaginary hair and tucked it behind her ear. "I want to be professional, Barrett. It's my first job, and I don't want anyone here thinking, you know…"

Standing up from my desk, I walked toward her and kissed her chastely on the mouth. "Tell me again why we have to keep our relationship a secret?" I asked, already drunk on her lips.

The tops of her cheeks glowed blush pink. I inhaled her vanilla floral scent, loving how she was just as affected as me with one kiss, one look, and one touch.

"Connor's got a lot on his plate, and my parents are bickering… I just want to enjoy our bubble as long as we can before we let the world in."

A knock at the door startled her, and she automatically pulled away from me.

"Barrett." Olivia's voice echoed through the crack of the door.

"To be continued, dollface." I winked, then returned to my desk. "Olivia, come in."

"You called?" Olivia walked in, taking in Lourde, a pink hue still evident on her silky skin.

"Olivia, meet Lourde Diamond. She'll be helping you on the Brooklyn townhomes for two weeks. She has a killer eye for detail and knows the wants and needs of our wealthy clientele."

"Nice to meet you, Lourde." Olivia shook her hand. "What a relief to have someone help us on such short notice."

"You too, Olivia. I'll surely try my best to help you where I can. I don't have any formal qualifications in interior design but–"

Olivia flapped her hand in the air, cutting her off.

"Whether you studied or not doesn't really matter. I saw the spread *Vogue* did in your home. I loved everything about it."

"Thank you, I actually had a bit of a say in that, much to Mom's dismay! She hired decorators and stylists but, in the end, went for what I suggested."

"I didn't know that, Lourde."

She turned and smiled, then a veil of professionalism replaced it. "I'm sure Connor must have mentioned it at some point."

"He may have. Olivia, don't burn out Lourde like you did Jessica, okay?"

Olivia narrowed her eyes. "I didn't burn her out. Maybe she just didn't have the temperament for the job."

I couldn't help but notice Lourde's mouth split into a grin, disguising it momentarily by taking her hand to her mouth. Did she like it that Olivia wasn't afraid of me? *Ha.*

She had noticed the fleet of staff that could double as *Sports Illustrated* models, but she wasn't threatened by Olivia. *Good.* Olivia was attractive, but with our constant back and forth, she was more like a sister. Then there was the hard-line I never ever crossed of sleeping with an employee. Connor, Ari, and Magnus thought I was crazy when they'd come to visit me for lunch, but Scout's honor, that part was true. I'd worked too damn hard to fuck it up on a one-night stand and lawsuit.

I liked to look at pretty women, or should I say, I used to. Looking didn't make me a villain. What made me a villain was seeing my mother's lifeless, dead body surrounded by a pool of blood with the gun still in my hands.

"Barrett, are you okay?" Olivia asked. "You're ghost white."

I blinked back to reality, both women staring at me

with concern. "I'm fine. Give us a minute, Olivia. I will send Lourde your way in just a moment."

"Sure. See you soon, Lourde," Olivia said, turning to walk out. Lourde missed the side glance Olivia shot my way, but I didn't. *Fuck!* Let her think whatever she wants. She shut the door behind her.

"I like her."

I laughed. "I thought you might. Olivia has been here the longest, and I trust her implicitly. But I don't think that's why you're fond of her, is it?"

She smirked. "I like how she doesn't stare at you like you're man-candy. And she's not afraid to speak up. I get the feeling few people do that to you."

"Do I come across as Mr. Unapproachable?" I rounded the desk and reached for her hands, pulling her into me.

"That's one word."

"Oh, go on, please."

She twisted her lips. "Mysterious."

Unexpected but okay.

"Where did you go before? One minute you were with us talking, and the next, you were in your head."

I leaned back on the edge of the table, creating a little space between us but interlacing my fingers with hers. Telling Lourde about my past was one thing, but having her think of me as a monster was something that could break us, and I just couldn't let that happen.

"All you need to know is that my past wasn't rainbows and unicorns. You know about my sister, Evelyn, needing care, and my parents are dead. Memories just come back, sometimes when I least expect it."

Her face softened. "Barrett, I'm here for you. I just wish you'd open up."

"Maybe one day, but right now, all I need is you. You're the light to my dark, Lourde." I leaned in, tilting her chin up and brushing my lips across hers. I gripped her waist with the other hand, pressing her into my groin.

She wrapped her hands around my neck and deepened the kiss before suddenly pulling away.

"Barrett, we shouldn't," she said, smoothing down her skirt and taking a step back.

"No one knows anything," I said, adjusting myself.

Her gaze lowered to the bulge in my pants.

"I think Olivia might suspect something."

"Nonsense." But even I doubted my own words. "Speaking of Olivia, you better go. I think she's heading out to Brooklyn, and I'm late for my next meeting."

"Whoops, see, you're a distraction! By the way, did you hear back from the detectives about the fire at 21 Park?"

"Yes, Detective Summer called. All evidence definitely points to arson."

"Damn, do they have any leads?"

"It's sold, so it's not really my problem, but it leaves an unpleasant taste in my mouth. I've got my team investigating."

"Your team?"

"From a young age, I've learned to only rely on myself, so if I need to find something out, it's on me, no one else. "

"So you have your own CSI squad?"

"Not quite. I have my two main guys, Jesse is ex-CIA, and Barton is ex-military, and if we need anything further, we have plenty of resources."

"I see. Well, luckily, no one was hurt. Let me know if I can help. I'm here for you. You know that, right?"

"I know. Hey, can we have dinner tonight?"

"I'd love that, but I've got the movers over at Tribeca moving me in, so I should probably unpack tonight."

"Girl's gotta eat. Let me bring over some takeout? I'd offer to cook, but I don't want you getting food poisoning."

"Me neither, and I'd love that, Barrett." She smiled, and the darkness inside disappeared for a moment.

"Okay, I really should go. I don't want Olivia thinking I'm slacking off on day one!"

She let go of my hands, but I pulled her back into me for a long kiss goodbye.

"To be continued tonight," I said with hooded eyes.

"Yes, please," she whispered before disappearing out of my office.

* * *

As the elevator ascended to Lourdes' apartment, I reflected on my last meeting of the day with my lawyers discussing the purchase of a Hamptons hotel. The trio of board members—Simon, Cary, and John—tried everything to wriggle out of the deal. They knew I had them by the balls when my team uncovered millions missing from the hotel and covered it up by firing hundreds of staff, sighting losses. Their indiscretions caught up with them in the end, and they finally relinquished, now signing it over for a steal.

The elevator doors opened, and I walked out carrying the two large paper bags of takeout I picked up on the way over. Not knowing what Lourde felt like eating, I basically ordered the entire menu from Nobu.

Like clouds unmasking pure sunshine, Lourde appeared around the corner in matching peach sweats and her golden-brown hair dusting the tips of her shoulders. "I've missed you." I put the bags down on the kitchen counter, and when I turned, she wrapped her arms around my neck, pushing her mouth to mine in a breathless kiss.

I groaned in response. "Have you? Do you know how hard it was concentrating at that desk?"

She giggled. "Maybe I ought to buy you a new desk then."

I pulled her close, so my cheek rested against hers, and my mouth grazed the shell of her ear. "Don't you dare." She pulled me tighter in response, her breath heavy. After a few more moments, we came up for air.

"Nice place." It was a cozy apartment with luxurious finishes, oak floors, and floor-to-ceiling windows over the Hudson River. Spread out on the floor beside half-pieced-together furniture were ornaments, books, and candles packaged in bubble wrap. Most of her things had already been unpacked with only a handful of items remaining.

It made me think back to my first apartment when I moved to Manhattan. Small was being too kind. Rusty taps, barely running water, peeling walls, and exposing moldy walls summed it up. But it was better than the long commute back home to Providence each day to see Evelyn or the crummy hostel in Manhattan where I slept when I was too exhausted to go back to Boston.

"Don't you have people to do this for you?" I picked up the screwdriver and Allen key by the box.

"They've done a lot already, but this is the stuff that I like to do. They don't know what's important to me and what's not. Plus, someone I don't know sorting out my belongings is a little impersonal, don't you think?"

"I couldn't agree more." I picked her up with ease, twirled her around then popped her back down.

"I am so hungry!" Spotting the paper bags I placed on the kitchen counter, she ravaged through them. She took out each neatly packed container, spreading them out on the marble counter. "You know there's only two of us, right?"

"I know, but I couldn't help but think you might be hungry."

"I am hungry," she said, eyeing the kingfish sashimi. "I don't know where the plates are."

"That's okay. Once upon a time, take out was a luxury, so eating out of containers isn't a big deal for me," I said.

She stopped what she was doing and regarded me. The look she gave me was one I knew to mean she was unsure. Truth was, these little snippets into my past just came out without thinking. She seemed to have that effect on me. The more we were around each other, the more my guard came down.

"I don't even have wine glasses," she said, and I was thankful she didn't press for more.

I held up the vintage bottle of red to my lips, pretending to take a swig. A laugh escaped her bow-shaped lips, her hazel eyes lighting up with humor.

"I think we have exchanged enough bodily fluids not to worry about drinking out of a bottle."

"You're right there, gorgeous."

"Maybe we can share a bit more than wine later?" she asked, dragging her teeth across her lips as she handed me a container of food.

"Are you asking me or telling me, dollface?"

"Ah… telling."

"Good girl." Warmth shot up my legs in anticipation of tracing every inch of her body. I took the container from her hand and cornered her with my gaze. "First, we shall eat because you will need energy for what I want to do to you on every surface of this new home of yours."

A hue of crimson spread toward her chest to her neck and matched the heat in my pants. Having her pop in and out of the office today but not being able to touch her and bend her over my desk was driving me crazy.

* * *

We threw away all the containers, and she seemed to be thankful for the easy cleanup.

"And you didn't think we could get through it all. There's only one dish remaining." I popped an eyebrow and tossed her the tea towel.

"What can I say? You know what I like."

"I think I do." My voice came off husky.

She leaned so her back was against the kitchen counter and folded her arms across her body. "So, what do I want right this minute?"

"You want me to fuck you, hard."

She blushed again, tilting her chin down. I wasn't going to let her get away with that so easily. I pushed my body against hers, holding her chin between my thumb and forefinger as I stared into her gorgeous hazels.

"You want it rough, dollface?"

She nodded.

"Do you remember the first time I asked you to touch yourself in the Hamptons? I want you to do the same now. Show me what I do to you," I commanded.

"What?" she mumbled out on a shallow breath.

"Your body is like a dirty sin meant for me, Lourde. I want to see you in all your glory."

"But I want you to touch me." She pouted.

"In time, dollface. Touch yourself... *now*."

5

LOURDE

My breath grew shallow as his hand in mine slid inside my sweats. Instead of being embarrassed this time, I watched his heated gaze on mine as I pleasured myself. Heat pooled in my core as I dragged my gaze down to the bulge in his suit pants.

He lowered his pants and started stroking himself. His biceps flexed as he clasped his large hands around the base, pulling it to the tip.

Fuck, watching him get off was the hottest thing. Now I understood. Gasping for air, I came for him while watching him stroke himself slowly and sensually.

He let go of himself and dropped to his knees, pulling my sweats down. He darted his tongue between my thighs, pulling another orgasm from me until I whimpered in delight and exhaustion.

"Barrett," I rounded out his name on a moan.

He came to stand and held out his hand. I took his lead and somehow made it to the bedroom. With haste, we both peeled off our clothes, tossing them to the floor.

"Lie on your stomach," he ordered in that dirty, husky voice that made me weak at the knees.

I did as he asked and heard the tearing of a foil packet and the snap of rubber.

He clung onto my hips, then without warning, slammed into me, so deep it propelled me forward, and I put my hands down to counterbalance the force.

"Do you like that, dollface?"

"Yes, fuck, yes," I groaned.

His finger lightly touched my back entrance. And every nerve ending stood on end. "How about this?"

I looked back, and with his hand at the base of his cock, he dragged our juices up wetting me, *there*.

The cool sensation had me fisting the sheets in my hands, absorbing the delicious burn.

"Do you want this?"

I groaned, unable to find words.

"Tell me, dollface."

"Yes! I want it."

He didn't hesitate and dipped his finger inside my back entrance. *Fuck yes.*

I squeezed my lady parts—the fullness, his fullness everywhere, making me orgasm in waves clamping down around him.

A few thrusts later, he found his release, then slumped on my back. "Sweet fuck, Lourde."

"I don't think I'll ever get bored with you." I breathed out.

"Well, I like the sound of that," he said, stroking the tender skin around the curve at the side of my breast. "So…"

"So?"

"How was your very first day at work today?" He rolled me over, and I sat upright.

"Busy, but so good. I can see why Olivia needs help. She has her team, but even with them, she's run off her feet with all the projects you have for her."

Mirroring me, he slid up against the tan leather headboard. "She can handle it."

"She's great," I said. "The Brooklyn site is still an array of contractors, kitchens at different levels, bathrooms at various stages, and it's being finished in less than two weeks?"

"Guess so."

"You don't seem worried about it."

"Olivia's on it. With you, why worry? It only ages you unnecessarily."

"I can see why you're so successful. Calm under pressure is a unique trait to have. Connor certainly doesn't possess it." She laughed.

"What's up with Connor? He has been partying a little harder than usual lately. I noticed that in the Hamptons."

"To be honest, I'm not too sure. But I think it has something to do with Dad's impending retirement and Connor taking over the reins."

"Big shoes to fill there," Barrett said, his hand falling to below my waist.

"Uh-huh." I breathed, uncertain if my body could take another Barrett-induced orgasm, let alone if I could walk straight tomorrow.

His hand stroked the inside of my thigh, and my skin tingled with excitement.

"Are you handy with a screwdriver?" I said, and he stopped his stroking.

"Are you trying to talk dirty, dollface?"

I threw my head back in laughter. "Hardly." I picked up the screwdriver on the half-put-together bedside table and handed it to him.

"Oh, shit, no."

Barrett's lighthearted laughter filled me with happiness. "What happened to the movers?"

"They forgot this piece, I guess." I shrugged and pulled up my sweats and tee.

He sat naked on my bed, looking too funny with a tented sheet and a screwdriver in hand.

"Only because it's you, Lourde." He rolled off the bed, slipped his pants on so they hung off his hips, and pulled on his shirt.

I watched him methodically piece together the side table. He effortlessly talked to me while working on the complex drawer structure and putting it in place.

"I could get used to this." Domesticated Barrett could be even hotter than business-tycoon Barrett.

He smiled an enormous smile. "So could I." He pinned his green eyes on mine, and I pictured it all—him staring down the altar as I walked toward him, declaring his love and our happily ever after. He glanced away, and my dreams disappeared as quickly as they came.

"So we haven't discussed what you'd like to be paid for your time at ZF Construction."

Where did he go in that brief space between happily ever after and now? And why was his tone suddenly so serious?

"What?" I asked, perplexed by the change of man.

"Your two weeks."

"I don't care to be paid. It's experience."

He tilted his head. "Nonsense."

"Honestly. I'm not even qualified. Just let me help you, and if Olivia thinks I have any shred of talent, then we can talk."

"Okay, only if you're sure?"

"I'm sure."

"Okay. This is done," he said, screwing in the last handle and standing the side table upright.

"Thank you. Will you stay the night?"

"I didn't bring an overnight bag."

"Oh, of course. I understand," I said, wishing he had thought to pack something.

"Plus, I don't know how much sleep we would truly get now if I stayed." His heated gaze trailed the corners of my mouth.

"True," I said, no less disappointed.

His tall frame engulfed me in a firm hug. Hands dipped to below my waist as his lips brushed across mine in a long, crushing kiss.

I kissed him back with a desperation I could only have for him.

"If I don't go now, I'll never go."

"Is that a bad thing?" I asked, fluttering my eyelids, and I watched his Adam's apple bob up and down.

"If you want to be bad, come by my office at one and wrap those delicious lips where they belong."

My mouth fell open at his proposition, and a grin lifted on his lips.

"Till tomorrow, dollface." With that, he turned and walked out of my apartment.

* * *

"That actually works," Olivia said, admiring my wallpaper selection against the already installed furniture.

"It's not something I'd think to pick, but the contrast works."

"Thanks," I said, packing away the other samples. "I'll get it to the contractors immediately," I said.

"Perfect."

"How about some lunch?" Olivia asked.

"I can't. I have to head back. I have a meeting with Barrett," I said, turning around so she couldn't see the blush climbing my neck.

"No problem, another time then."

"Absolutely, I'd love to."

"So tell me why you're here."

I spun around. "What do you mean?"

"You don't have to work, Lourde. Your family is up there with the Rockefellers. I hope you don't mind me stating the obvious."

I laughed. "No, you're right. I just wanted a different choice."

"How so?"

"One where I wasn't the prize. I want to contribute, maybe even excel at something."

"Oh, I hear you. Why can't we make something out of ourselves? And why are men threatened by a woman with a career?" She shook her head.

"Is that what you've found?" I asked, wanting to know more about Olivia.

Her hair was blonde in a long bob, her eyes puffy but still bright blue.

"Oh, I have shares in every dating app out there. For weeks at a time, I'd go on morning, lunch, and evening dates just to find the one. Some worked out. Most didn't. And what it came down to was me, married to my job."

"That's rough."

"They're just threatened, is all. Why would I leave all this? Not when I've helped Barrett create it."

"Absolutely."

"And for what? A lousy lay! Heck, I'm twenty-eight years old. I need a man who knows what he's doing!"

I laughed. "Sorry, I shouldn't laugh. I've just met all those men. They're all douchebags."

"So, are you dating now?"

I cleared my throat. "I just broke it off with my ex, so no." I was a terrible liar.

"Oh, I saw that in the papers a few weeks ago. And I'm assuming you know Barrett through your brother, Connor, right?"

"Yes, they've been friends for years. Barrett actually sold our family one of our condos when he was working for another property developer in his first job in the city."

"Well, he's certainly come a long way since then!"

"Speaking of Barrett, I better head off."

"Sure thing. I'll see you later. Good work today, Lourde."

I smiled, and I knew she wasn't blowing smoke up my skirt. "Thank you!"

"Now go on, you don't want to leave the boss waiting."

I blushed. "No, of course not."

Not for what I have planned.

6

BARRETT

I wasn't dreaming, was I?

Saying nothing, she locked the door behind her, slid onto my lap, and hitched up her pencil skirt, devouring my lips in a kiss laced with desire. Hot and breathy tongues fought for domination, and a moan escaped my lips when she ground down against my thickening cock.

Tilting her head back, I traced the underside of her earlobe with kisses, down to her blouse that popped open, exposing her porcelain cleavage clothed in the emerald lace bra she knows drives me crazy.

"Ah no, you don't." Moaning, she lifted my chin up and out of her delicious tits, then she kneeled between the gap of my chair and desk, pulling me closer to her, so the desk completely hid her from sight, with only a slight gap for my viewing pleasure. She unzipped my pants and grabbed my thickness with both hands, stroking me between her fingertips.

"Fuck, dollface, I could get used to seeing this every lunchtime," I moaned as I shuffled to the edge of the chair, her hand roughly sliding up and down my shaft, my length impossibly long with her touch. She swiped her tongue over my length, and heat shot up my thighs.

I wrapped my hands around her head and leaned back, watching her show.

She sucked me, warm and wet, clasping her lips around my shaft and... "Holy fuck!" I leaned forward, gripping the edge of the desk with one hand for support as she took me down her delicious throat, deep-throating me. Then again.

I felt her grin around my cock, and the sensation set my body on fire.

"Lourde, you're something else," I said.

She moaned around my cock, and the sound reverberated up my shaft.

My toes tingled, and my brow broke out into beads of sweat. "Lourde, I'm going to come."

The phone buzzer pinged loudly.

"Fuck!" I groaned out, but she was relentless, not stopping, instead pushing me deeper down her throat just to unnerve me.

It buzzed again, and I hit the button so it was on speaker. "What is it, Aimee?" I bit out in a strained voice.

Unfettered, Lourde cupped my balls, and with one last rake of her teeth over my cock, I exploded, shooting my hot liquid down her throat and slamming my fists on the table as I came.

"Sir, is everything okay?"

"Yes, fine."

"Right. I have Connor Diamond here to see you. He says it's urgent."

Fuck!

A thud underneath the table sounded, followed by a faint moan.

"Sir?"

"Yes."

"Shall I send him in?" Aimee questioned.

"Give me a minute."

I hung up and looked down. Lourde's eyes were the size of saucers as she rubbed the crown of her head.

"What the hell, Barrett?" she whispered.

"Just stay down. He can't see you there." I stroked her jaw and quickly kissed her on the mouth before she retreated under the desk. I tucked myself in and zipped up. Standing quickly, I pushed my chair underneath the desk, concealing her from view.

I ran a hand through my brow, wiping the sweat that popped up, then unlocked the door.

"Connor."

He pushed past me and into the room. *Did it smell like cum?*

"What are you doing here?" I said, trying to pretend his sister's lips weren't just around my cock, giving me epic head.

He sat down on the seat opposite mine, and I closed the door before I made my way over to my chair. Carefully sliding it back, I shot a quick glance down where she sat on her knees, statue-still.

"Thank fuck you're here, Barrett. I just had to get out. I'm going insane!"

I sat down, casting my eyes over him. "What's wrong? You look terrible."

"My father. That's what's wrong,"

"What's Alfred done?"

"It's what he hasn't." He threw his hands in the air. "He expects me to take over the media empire but doesn't trust me, going behind my back or micromanaging me, so I'm second-guessing myself. I just can't handle it."

"Isn't he just checking in on you?"

"No, it's way worse than that." Connor put his head in his hands.

"What are you going to do?" I asked, trying to wrap this up. I hadn't seen him like this before, but now was certainly not the time to delve deep with my cock still wet from his sister's mouth.

"I don't know. I just don't know."

"Hey, I know. How about after work tonight, we call the boys and get together, blow a bit of steam off?"

"Yeah, sorry man, to barge in on you," he said, looking around then taking me in. "You all right?"

"Perfect, just busy."

"Of course you are. Fuck, I sound like a pussy."

"Connor, you don't sound like a pussy. Okay, maybe a little, but shit, man, you've got your old man breathing down your neck. That is not an ideal situation. Pressure is a motherfucker, and you've got the king breathing down on you."

I stood up. And thankfully, he followed my lead. "You, me, the boys, see you at eight at Sky Deck?"

I rounded the desk and put my hand on his shoulder, leading him toward the door.

"Done. Thanks for listening."

"Of course."

I opened the door and watched him walk away. Once I was sure he was gone, I shut it and locked it once more. I leaned against the back of the door and exhaled. *That was way too close.*

She crawled out, her eyes wide. "Barrett, that was too close," she said, leaning against the desk.

"I was thinking the same thing." I walked over to her and sat where Conner was just seated.

"We should just tell him, Lourde."

"Are you serious? Didn't you hear him? He sounded awful. I don't know what kind of pressure Dad has him under, but adding our relationship to the mix certainly wouldn't help right now."

"Are you sure that's the only reason?"

"Of course." She walked toward me and perched her ass up on the edge of the desk, her heels brushing my Italian shoes.

My gaze fell to her lips, and she flapped the corner of her blouse. "Is it warm in here?" she asked.

"It's about to be."

The buzzer sounded again, and I groaned.

"Busy man." She widened her eyes.

I cut a chaste kiss across her jaw, then moved round, pressed the flashing button. "What is it?"

"I have Sam here."

"I don't have a construction meeting scheduled with Sam today."

"I know, he says it's urgent. There's a crane malfunction."

"Right." I hung up and kissed Lourde on the mouth. "I'm sorry. I'll make it up to you."

"I know you will." She smoothed down her skirt as she stepped off the edge of the desk and walked beside me toward the door. "Later?"

"Definitely." I squeezed her hand before letting it go and quietly unlocked the door.

"Thank you, Barrett. I'll ensure the contractors are on it."

She gave magnificent head and could keep a part. "Good, we want to be ahead of the game."

She nodded, then turned, not before I noticed a slight smile pull from the corner of her lips.

"Thank you, Aimee." Her confused look at the appearance of Lourde exiting my office was priceless.

Hiding Lourde's arrival was easy when you sent your assistant away for lunch.

"Sam. What can I do for you?"

Sam strolled in, curiosity forming a grin on his plump cheeks. "Is Lourde Diamond working for us?"

"She's helping Olivia now that Jessica just quit."

I shut the door.

"Well, she's a breath of fresh air around here," he said.

A vein throbbed in my neck. Sam was always eyeing up the younger employees, and more than once, I had to interfere with behavior that was borderline harassment.

"We have a massive problem in Soho. The crane carrying a haul of metal beams dropped from three stories high."

"What the fuck? Is everyone okay?"

"Paramedics have just arrived and picked up two of the crew with some collateral damage, a few broken bones, but no deaths. Luckily, no one was directly underneath."

"Why the fuck aren't you there? Let's go. You can fill me in on the way," I said, not bothering to grab my jacket and wanting to get there and work out exactly how this could happen when we run one of the tightest, safest worksites in all of Manhattan.

The fire and now this? A sinking feeling in the pit of my stomach ignited.

Something wasn't right.

* * *

"You made it," Conner said, already seated with the boys at Sky Deck, overlooking the glow of Central Park below.

"By the look of you, I think you should get that man a drink," Ari said, taking me in.

I raked a hand through my hair. "Make it a bottle," I said. The sinking feeling hadn't left me. It had only grown stronger when we went to Soho. The crane's metal package lay in a twisted ruin on the site. Solid structural metal beams had fallen, and the crane operator had no idea why it occurred. None of his equipment had malfunctioned, which meant either they did not secure the package properly or someone tampered with the braiding cable.

"What happened, Barrett? I heard it on the news on the way over," Magnus asked.

"I'm still getting to the bottom of it. But I think someone tampered with the cable."

"What? Why would someone do that?" Conner asked.

"I don't know. But first, there was the fire at 21 Park, and now this." I shook my head. "I don't believe in coincidences."

"Shit, man. That's crazy if that's the case," Ari said.

"I know." I poured three fingers of scotch and drank it down in one long gulp.

I slammed the tumbler down, and three sets of eyes took me in.

"We're here for you, buddy," Connor said, slapping me between the shoulder blades.

A slash of guilt tingled up my spine, but I couldn't deal with that right now.

"Have you got the police working on anything?" Ari inquired.

"I've got my own team who get me answers quicker than the police ever could."

"Good idea," Connor said.

"Aren't the sites locked down each night?" Ari asked.

"Yes, and I've got security on them twenty-four-seven. I

have more security and safety measures in place than any other construction company." I poured another three fingers. "Which makes me think maybe it could be an inside job."

"Jesus Christ, Barrett," Magnus huffed out.

"Are you safe, man?" Ari leaned forward, concern on his face.

"I couldn't care less about my safety. But the person fucking with me and my business sure as fuck should be worried."

"Makes my dramas seem trivial in comparison," Conner said. "Sorry to barge in on you today. I could tell you had a lot going on."

"That's fine, Connor."

"Did I hear your sister is working for you, Barrett?" Magnus asked, and my chin nearly hit the floor.

"Lourde? What the hell, Barrett?"

"Actually, I was going to tell you today, but it slipped my mind. She's just helping on the interiors of the Brooklyn townhomes, seeing my second-in-charge just quit and basically ghosted all of us."

He narrowed his eyes at me, piercing blues questioning me behind hooded eyes.

"Why Lourde?"

"She's always liked design, so it was a good fit. It's only short-term till she figures out what she really wants to do."

"I thought it was a Diamond policy that no women could work," Magnus questioned.

"Yeah, well, Dad changed her mind on that. Seems he's changed his mind on a lot of things lately. I wonder why she didn't tell me?"

I shrugged. "Can't tell you."

Ari regarded me, not believing me for a second, then

changed the subject completely. Fucker knew me too damn well.

"Connor, I received an invitation to the annual Diamond Charity Ball."

He groaned. "Oh, fabulous."

"Got mine," Magnus said.

"Mine too." I grinned, hoping by then we could be out and proud of our relationship in the next three weeks.

7

LOURDE

The last few days were a whirlwind of managing contractors for the eight kitchen installations in the Brooklyn townhouses, unpacking and sorting the last of my things, and planning a housewarming party.

"What a week!" Olivia said, stopping by my temporary desk. "If it wasn't for your help this week, Lourde, I think these fine lines would be deep crevices." She pointed to the corners of her eyes, where, honestly, there wasn't a line in sight.

I laughed, but hell, I should thank her. For once, it was nice to be a valued member of a team. Prior to this, I'd never had to work for anything, and my purpose was lacking unless I wanted to be a permanent charity ball planner—which I certainly did not.

"I'm loving it," I said truthfully.

She arched a perfectly plucked eyebrow. "Really?"

"Absolutely. The fast pace, the hardhats toeing the line with politeness versus being direct with the contractors so they get the job done properly... all of it. I love It."

"Okay! This job does suit you."

I shrugged. "Guess so."

She eyed me. "Or maybe it's the people here. I'm not sure which," Olivia said, sitting at the edge of my desk, tapping her fingers on the swatch samples I had fanned out like a color wheel.

Shit, she knows. How could she possibly know?

"Definitely the job."

A grin rose into the corners of her mouth. "If you say so."

"I do!" I pressed, trying to sound as convincing as I could.

"Barrett looks at you…" she paused before opening her mouth again, "… differently."

"Well, I've known him for such a long time. He's friends with Connor so…"

Why was she still staring at me with that shit-eating grin on her pretty face?

She folded the color wheel back together. "Well, the girls around here have definitely upped their game since you arrived."

I glanced up at her. "What? How can they up their game? They're all models. Does Barrett just hire beautiful women?"

"Ha! I certainly don't put myself in that category."

"Well, you ought to. You're a stunner, Olivia."

"Yeah, well, it's a pity men are threatened by a successful woman. But regarding your question, Barrett does like looking at beautiful things. Whether they are lines of a building or women."

My chest heaved even though he said there was no one else but me. Temptation was all around him.

"But in his defense, he's fired all the inept workers. The ones who work here can actually do their job."

"So they are smart and beautiful… great," I said through gritted teeth.

"And by the looks of the higher heels and shorter skirts this week, they've noticed you, Lourde. Or should I say, noticed you pulling the boss's attention?"

Heat stretched across my shoulder blades up to my neck. I had gotten close to Olivia this week, but even so, keeping our relationship under wraps, for now, was in everyone's best interests. I could actually imagine Pepper and Grace liking Olivia too, but regardless, I couldn't tell her about Barrett and me. Not until I told Connor.

"Ladies, what are we discussing over here that's so important?" His dark voice settled in the crevices of my belly.

"There you are," Olivia said.

I stared up from my seat, and his eyes softened when meeting mine. Fuck, I'd missed him the last few days. Like a hurting, heaving ache to the artery.

"Just talking about the intelligent women who work here," Olivia said, letting out a chuckle.

He took her in curiously, then glanced toward me. I lowered my gaze, filing away the folders on my desk for fear of being caught.

"I think you're feeding Lourde nonsense. Go home. Get laid, Olivia, and enjoy the weekend off."

"Ha! I think I've scared all the men in Manhattan away. Might have to go to Long Island to find me a real man."

"Shit… poor bastards." Barrett laughed.

"Smartass," she tsked.

"Do you always talk to each other like that?" I asked like a spectator enjoying the duel playing out in front of me

"Like what?" Barrett questioned, completely oblivious.

Olivia rolled her eyes. "Mostly, yeah, but considering

the fucktard of a week you've had, Barrett, you've been in a particularly good mood."

Barrett stood calmer than the Dalai Lama while a blush swept across my chest, clawing at the base of my neck. One of these days, my damn skin was going to out me if I couldn't figure out a way to get myself under control.

Her mouth curled into a knowing smile that trumped any rebuttal Barrett surely had. "Well, if I have the weekend off, I'm getting the hell out of here."

"Who are you kidding, Olivia? You'll be checking your emails every five minutes." She looked over her shoulder and frowned.

"Enjoy your weekend, you two." She smirked and walked away.

"Hmm… I think she may be onto us," Barrett said, lowering his mouth to my ear, his stubble brushing against my jaw. There were only a few people left in the office, and I knew Barrett was watchful of curious eyes.

"I think so too." I wanted him to trace me with kisses and taste me with his expert tongue. I didn't care if it got us caught. I needed his hands on my body.

I pressed into his jaw scrub. "I've missed you," I said.

He pulled back from the side of my face and tilted his head down, his hooded eyes chained to mine. I watched his Adam's apple bob up and down as he traced my lips with his molten gaze.

Heat pooled at the base of my stomach. "Come home with me, Lourde?" His words came out with aching need that matched mine.

"I was hoping you'd say that."

* * *

As soon as the doors closed to his private elevator, his hands immediately skimmed my thigh, finding their way between my legs. He pressed me against the wall with the weight of his body while his fingers hooked inside me, and my head tipped back against the mirrored wall.

My phone rang in my hand, and we both looked at the name flashing on the screen.

I groaned, taking him to my lips in a sinful kiss and ignoring my brother's phone call.

"Answer it, "Barrett said, with his fingers still inside of me.

"What?" I gasped, nearly choking on my surprise.

Something in his eyes dared me, but he wasn't removing his fingers. He kept them in there, pleasuring me, deliciously.

"I'm breathless with you inside me."

"So?"

Fuck it. "Connor, what's up?" I answer an octave too high.

Barrett dragged his teeth across my neck, nipping a fold of skin between them, making me gasp. Quickly, I put my hand over my mouth.

"What's up? When were you going to tell me you got a job working for Barrett?"

At the mention of his name, Barrett's fingers plunged quicker into me—fuck, three fingers now and…

oh…

shit…

answer the damn question, Lourde.

"No big deal," I said, my voice coming off strained. Barrett took that moment to put his finger in my mouth, and I bit down on a hiss.

"You sound weird. Where are you?"

Harder and faster, his fingers fucked me until I was on the edge. "Just busy. I'll see you tomorrow."

Making sure I clicked the off button, I groaned out my release in a satisfactory and hungry orgasm, dropping the phone and gripping onto his strong shoulders as I came in waves around him.

"You bad girl," he said, pulling his fingers out of me and taking them to his nose, breathing in my scent.

I slapped his shoulders hard. "I'll get you back for that."

"Oh, I hope you do," he said, pulling out from my claw hug and chasing my gasp with a kiss.

After a moment, we disentangled. I hadn't noticed the elevator doors were open.

He picked up my phone that I'd dropped when I was overcome with overwhelming pleasure and both our briefcases. "Come with me." His voice was husky with an unmet need.

Knowing he wasn't done with me yet, exhilaration shot up the base of my spine, even with jelly legs, as I walked into his apartment. He stopped at the kitchen counter and dropped both bags, where they landed with a thud against the tiled flooring.

"Where do you want me?" I purred.

"Dollface, I want to fuck you anywhere I can, whenever I can. But right now, I want to rip that tight black skirt you have on and fuck you over my countertop."

Oh, that dirty mouth. I loved it.

Saying nothing, I brushed past him toward the shorter edge of the counter. Leaving my heels and skirt on, I bent onto my elbows, resting them on the counter, and spread my legs apart teasingly slow. Still raw from the orgasm he pulled before, I felt sexier than fucking ever and his. *All his.*

"Mmm, now there's a sight," he said. "I've been thinking about this moment way too much."

With one hand, he gently but firmly pressed down on my back so my chest was now laying against the cool surface, then nudging my legs apart further with his polished Italian shoe, I spread open for him.

My heated skin tingled against the chilled marble counter as my nipples stiffened beneath my blouse.

With one hand, he reached underneath my skirt, feeling the remnants of my wetness.

"Your cunt is perfect," he said as he slid his fingers through my wet folds and into me once more.

I groaned at his dirty, husky words.

"What are you waiting for?" I questioned.

"Impatient are we, dollface?"

I nodded, aching for him to fill me from base to tip.

"Are you on birth control?"

I hadn't gone off it since my ex.

"Yes."

"And I'm clean."

He swirled his fingers inside of me, taking turns rubbing my clit with my wetness.

"Good, because I want to feel you. I want you to take what I have to give you, Lourde."

My pussy clamped down at his words.

And with one deft move, the metal swipe of his zipper sounded, followed by his pants falling. His hand inched up my skirt, pulling apart my lace thong. He teased me at the opening of my folds with his hard, thick tip.

"Barrett, please." I breathed out on a plea.

He dipped inside me slowly at first, and I pressed into the countertop. Free from the binds of latex, he was excruciatingly delicious.

"Oh, fuck, Lourde, you feel…" He plowed into me

again, and with the force of his thrust, my hips hit against the corner of the counter. His hands fell around my hips, between the sharp edge of the counter and my bones, protecting me, as he continued his tantric assault.

Blistering heat overcame me and flowed up my back, but I couldn't round out any words.

"Jesus Christ." His words hissed out between his teeth.

With my nipples rubbing against the cool counter, it was enough to tip me over the edge. "Barrett," I yelled as I saw a rainbow of stars.

With one last thrust, he spilled into me, his dick quivering inside me. I clamped down on him, wanting all he had to give me.

He rested his body on top of me, not giving me his full weight but a warm embrace as he remained inside me, his hand wrapped around my body. I turned my head so his breath was on my cheek.

"That was… I have no words for that, dollface."

"I love you, Barrett." The words left my mouth without realizing that's what I was going to say, but it was true—every word. I held my breath, waiting for him to say something. Anything. He stared at me long and hard, then took my mouth and kissed me in a long, slow kiss that if he wasn't pinning me upright, I think I would have slumped to the ground.

8

BARRETT

I woke up with an aching feeling in my chest. It wasn't Lorde splayed out with her vanilla-scented body wash and her hair across my bare chest, but rather the three little words that I couldn't say back to her—*I love you.* For the life of me, I couldn't get the words past my lips.

It wasn't because I didn't love her. I'd fallen for her so deeply it scared me like a crushing weight. I'd never felt this way before—mainly because no one had ever made me feel anything before Lourde came along. I was a one-night guy, and commitment wasn't in the realm of possibility. But with Lourde, all my walls came down. I didn't have a choice. The more I fought it, the more I couldn't be apart from her. Like a drug, I craved her, and without her, I was wandering around with my head in the sand.

I loved her so fucking much it hurt, but I just couldn't voice the words. Lourde deserved the world. I thought I could push away the guilt of my mom, but it still lingered like the metallic taste of blood on my tongue. Less so than before, but it was still there. She knew there was a secret buried and I wasn't giving her my all.

Still, she'd said, "I love you." The woman was remarkable, and here I was, fearing the worst. And at any moment, it could crash down and burn to hell. Just like Mom was taken from me, ripped away when I couldn't wrestle the gun from Dad's grip. Just like my sister, Evelyn, with her permanent gunshot injury to the thigh.

Lourde was perfect, but I feared I wasn't enough for her. She deserved more. One day she'd realize that. Then, as soon as she knew about my darkness, she'd run.

Who'd want to be with a monster like me?

The hole in my chest ached, and as though sensing my pain, she groaned, her hand rising to settle on my chest. Planting a kiss on her lips, I slid away quietly, sitting upright and shuffling out of bed.

I put on my gray sweats and headed out of the bedroom, pulling the door closed behind me.

* * *

With urgent emails now complete, the growls of an empty stomach superseded the dull ache in my chest. I wasn't the world's best cook, but I wanted to make Lourde breakfast. I'd learned a thing or two about meal preparation, and when I left Boston for Manhattan to work in property development, I learned the basics of cooking after very long days.

I opened the double Liebherr refrigerator doors, casting my eyes over the stocked shelves my housekeeper always kept full. Picking up Lourde's favorite yogurt then the fresh blueberries and strawberries and a bottle of Canadian maple syrup, I scanned the pantry shelf with neatly labeled clear containers and located the oats.

How hard could it be to toast oats in a pan? If I could

build a tower with half a billion, I could sure as fuck toast some oats.

Halving the strawberries, I threw them on top of the yogurt, then added a few blueberries on top for decoration. Now the oats. I poured them into the nonstick pan with a chunk of butter because heck, it was Saturday.

Shit, I hadn't called Evelyn. Typically, we'd try to talk every week on Saturday, but it was becoming less frequent these last few weeks.

I put the pan on the stove, slid my phone out of my pocket, and went to my favorites. A ring later and she was there.

"Barrett!"

"Hey, sis. Sorry I didn't call earlier. It's been crazy."

"When is it not crazy? I've been hearing about the fire, then the crane accident?"

"It's been hectic."

"Are you okay?" she asked, concerned.

"Actually, I'm fine. I couldn't be better apart from the work pressure."

"You sound different."

I smiled. "I'm with Lourde."

"What? Are you guys together now? Is she your girlfriend? The last conversation we had, you said you had a thing, but she was off to meet her future husband at some dinner."

"Okay, calm down, take a breath!" I laughed, but it was cute to see my sister excited for me. "Yes, she's my girlfriend. Fuck, well, I've never said that before."

"Ahh!" she screamed down the line so loud, I had to pull the phone away from my ear for a second.

"Evelyn, chill. God, you'd think you were sixteen again!"

"Wait, does Connor know?"

"No. I want to tell him, but Lourde is holding off. Connor's busy preparing for Alfred's retirement at Diamond Incorporated so she thinks the timing is off."

"Uh."

"Uh, what?"

"I'm so happy for you, brother, but I think the longer you leave it, the worse the outcome."

"I know. Maybe I'll convince her to tell him tonight. Lourde is having a housewarming, and he'll be there. But to be honest, I'm not sure if I can handle an irate Connor at the moment with everything else on my plate."

"What do you think he'd do?"

"I honestly don't know. But what *can* he do? We both want this. We're both consenting adults. I couldn't imagine my life without Lourde now that she's in it."

"Aww, I'm so happy for you, brother. You deserve all the happiness in the world and then some."

"Thanks, Eve. Tell me, how's the new physiotherapy?"

"It's hard to tell, but I think I'm improving."

"Good." I sighed. "Why don't you just come out to Manhattan?"

"Oh, you know me. I'm a creature of habit, and Boston's my home. But you never know, I might someday soon."

"I'd love that, Eve. I miss you. It's been too long."

"Miss you too, brother. So what's the update with 21 Park?"

"It's arson. But even though I'm no longer the owner, the detectives think it was a targeted attack on me."

"What? Who would do such a thing?"

"When there is money involved, I don't trust anyone."

"Barrett, I don't like the sound of this."

"It's fine. They won't hurt me. They are just interested in hurting my company, my brand, and my name."

64

"You're all I have left," she said, her voice thick and croaky.

"I'm not going anywhere, sis. Stop being dramatic."

"Okay, okay." She cleared her throat. "Please, just be careful."

"I'm fine. Those fuckers ought to look over their shoulder. Anyway, enough of that. I'd love to see you. Get your ass here, all right?"

Out of the corner of my eyes, Lourde appeared. "Morning, handsome," she said before noticing I was on the phone and mouthed the word *sorry*.

"Is that her?" Evelyn asked.

"Sure is," I said, admiring Lourde in her camisole and wild brown hair.

"Put her on."

"What?"

"You heard me, Barrett."

I settled for putting it on speaker.

"Lourde, meet Evelyn, my sister. She wanted to talk to you," I said, rolling my eyes.

"Oh, shush, Barrett. Hi, Lourde. Nice to meet you over the phone. I'm so happy you and Barrett are together."

I put my hand to my forehead. *How embarrassing.*

"Hey, Evelyn, nice to meet you too, and I'm so happy we're together too." She sent me a smile that hit me between the feels.

"Barrett said you live in Boston. Are you thinking of coming to New York soon?"

"I'm leaning toward a trip, yes."

"I could take you out if Barrett is busy, show you all the best places in Manhattan and have a girly day."

"Ooh, I'd love that." Evelyn's excitement was palpable, and it warmed me, hearing the two most important people in my life talking for the very first time.

I took Lourde's hand and pulled her onto my lap. She let out a squeal as she leaped forward, losing her balance. I caught her in my grasp and trailed kisses up her neck.

The piercing siren of the smoke alarm filled the room.

"Oh fuck, the oats!"

"Are you cooking?" I heard Evelyn ask, but I'd already shuffled Lourde to the side and ran into the kitchen.

"Got to go, Evelyn," I yelled over the noise. The golden oats were now crispy black and charcoal. *Dammit.* I fanned away the smoke billowing from the pan and opened the nearby window. After a minute, the deafening sound of the alarm was silenced.

Lourde appeared by my side. "Were you toasting oats?"

"I've seen them on your yogurt breakfast. I thought you might like them." She grazed her bottom lip with her top teeth. "You did this for me?"

Facing her, I raked a hand through my hair. "Well, it didn't work."

She pressed her body into me, wrapping her hands around my neck as she stepped up on her tippy toes. I wrapped my hands around her waist and pulled her closer to my chest.

"What are you smiling at, dollface?"

"I just love how you tried to make me breakfast," she said, staring down at the two bowls of Greek yogurt, chopped strawberries, and blueberries. "No man has ever made me breakfast before."

"It's burned."

"It's beautiful." Her eyes softened, and she made me forget the charcoal lumps and the pain in my heart.

"You're beautiful," I said, tucking a loose strand of hair and placing it behind the shell of her ear.

She blinked, and I drank her in, taking her lips in a possessive kiss. She kissed me back, deepening the kiss, squeezing her hands around my neck and pressing her groin into mine.

My dick responded, growing thick and hard and wanting a taste of her cunt.

I lowered my hands underneath her satin shorts and was delighted to find she was naked underneath. I cupped her smooth, bare ass and felt her moan into my mouth. Breathless, she stepped back and pulled down my sweats.

"Barrett, I need you."

I tipped her face up. Her eyes were needy and hungry like mine.

"Not here." I pulled up my sweats and led her out of the smokey kitchen and into the bathroom.

"You're dirty from last night," I said, stepping out of my sweats.

"I am?" she asked, pulling off her camisole, sliding down her shorts, and standing naked in my marble bathroom.

Slowly, I walked over to her as she cast her heated gaze down to the painfully large engorgement between my legs.

"Will I ever get enough of you, Lourde?"

She paused before looking up at me. "I hope not." I tilted her chin so she faced me. Her eyes were wet. *Just tell her you love her, you pussy.* "You are everything to me."

A slight smile appeared on her mouth.

It was too painful to see I'd let her down, so I lowered my mouth onto hers in a slow and possessive kiss. If I couldn't say the goddamn words, I needed to show her there was no one else but her.

I pulled her into the oversized glass-walled shower and turned the lever to a comfortably hot temperature. When I pinned her back against the marble wall, she shivered from the cool.

Lathering the soap between my hands until it resembled soft foam bubbles, I picked up the luffa. Steam billowed around us, and water cascaded like waterfalls off our naked bodies.

"I plan to wash my filth off you," I said, sliding the sponge down, around her hips, the curve of her ass, then back down the front of her, and around her belly.

She tilted her head back, absorbing the pressure of the scratchy luffa across her porcelain skin. My dick swelled, and I rubbed up against her thigh. I nipped at her jawline down to the column of her neck, tracing her collarbone while lathering her tits with foamy soap.

"I like your filth." She breathed out on a moan, taking my hair with her fist, so the roots tingled.

Her words had me pushing her thighs apart, gripping her legs, and wrapping them around me, plunging into her. She was more than ready, dripping wet for me.

"Fuck, dollface." I hissed into her neck, licking and tasting the water dripping from her hair.

"Oh God." She scrambled her legs higher, and I lifted her with my arm, so her legs crossed over my hips. I plunged deeper into her, the soap suds dripping down her breasts. My back radiated with heat, and my legs tensed.

"Kiss me," she demanded through a heavy breath, and my lips chased hers. Then, savagely, our tongues assaulted each other between gasps of breath and excruciating orgasmic sensations.

She opened her mouth and groaned.

"Say my name, dollface." With her eyes shut tight, her head against the tiles, and her hands in my hair, she screamed my name.

I croaked out a throaty groan as I found my release, spilling into her.

"I want more of that," she said breathlessly.

"Careful what you wish for," I said, gently lowering her legs to the tiled floor.

She opened her eyes. "Why?"

"Because I could fuck you all day long."

"What's wrong with that?" She lowered her lip, and fuck, she was ready for more.

"Don't tempt me," I said, stepping back from her purposely as I was so close to throwing it all to the wind today for her.

"I like tempting you, Barrett."

"I like it when you tempt me, but I have a meeting with my media team in twenty minutes, and don't you have a housewarming party to prepare for?"

"I do, yes," she said, not moving from her back against the wall and trailing my torso down to my dick.

"Let me wash you," she said, picking up the luffa, and without waiting for a reply, she lathered the soap in her hands and gripped my shaft.

"I said don't tempt me." With my cock in her velvet hands, I was her prisoner—one fucking happy prisoner. She glided my shaft, and it only took a few moments to lengthen again under her touch.

"I'm cleaning you," she said, gripping my ass and moving me under the stream of water, rinsing me off.

"Now you have me hard. What are you going to do about it?" I asked, arching an eyebrow.

"Fuck you with my mouth." She kneeled underneath the showerhead and pushed me against the wall. She swiped her tongue across my head and *Jesus, fuck.*

Her wet hair lengthened down her mid-back as she guided her bow lips around me. I raked a hand through my hair, letting her do whatever she pleased.

She started with long slow licks staring up at me.

Christ, fuck all meetings to hell.

She moaned as she took me deeper, deep throating me to the base of my groin while clutching my balls in her hand and giving me doe eyes.

Delicious lips wrapped around my cock, and I couldn't take it anymore. Gripping the back of her head, I guided her faster. With her hands at my base and her warm slippery lips around me moaning lightly, warmth spread throughout me as I shot my load down her throat.

"Fuck!" I croaked out on the waves of my orgasm, my legs heavy. I watched her wipe her mouth with the back of her hand, and it was hotter than hell.

"All clean," she said, running a finger along her bottom lip. I gripped her underneath her arms and held her up and into me, kissing her mouth in a breathless, needy kiss.

"Your fucking insatiable." I grinned.

"You love it." She smiled before something in her eyes held fear at the words she'd just spoken.

I blinked like a fucking deer in the headlights, and a blush crept up on her chest. She quickly glanced away and peeled her hand through her wet hair.

"I guess you have a meeting to get to. I don't want to hold you up anymore."

"Lourde, wait."

But she grabbed a towel and disappeared out the door.

"Fuck." I groaned, turning off the lever and resting my head on the tiles.

9

LOURDE

I don't know why I was so upset. Just because Barrett didn't say those three words back to me when I said them to him, it didn't mean he didn't love me, did it?

I loved him more than any goddamn thing in the world. With every single fiber of my being and in my soul's heart, he was the man for me. I knew it. I wanted him to know it and feel it too.

But the kicker was, I thought he loved me. It was in the depth of his kiss, his slow and desperate touch, and his need to fulfill me to try to make me breakfast by nearly burning the apartment down.

But now, with all my past heartache, I wondered if my feeling radar was way off.

The truth was, none of my ex-boyfriends compared to Barrett. Not one. It was embarrassing to call them exes because what I have with Barrett was ten times more than any of them combined.

This morning, I left Barrett after the shower and left him for his meetings. He had enough going on with managing the crane accident and juggling his PR response to the media that was crushing him with safety issues. So I let him be and returned to my apartment, helping prepare for tonight.

Hours later and now watching Pepper and Grace fuss about outfits to wear tonight, I couldn't wait to see him.

"Hey, love bug, stop thinking about his dick!"

"Jesus, Pepper!" I laughed.

"Well, was I right?" she pressed, turning around from my floor-length mirror to push me further.

I grinned. "You little slut bucket," Grace squealed. "But I'm so happy for you. Barrett is a catch among catches. Wait till the media gets wind of this. You two will be society's heaven."

I rolled my eyes. "I don't want that. I just want to hold on to us for as long as we can."

"Well, it's not going to go anywhere once the world knows."

"True." I pushed across the hangers, looking at my dresses for this evening—no, that wouldn't do. Nor would that.

The silence behind me made me stop what I was doing. Pepper was looking down at her phone. "Oh, my God. I knew it." She threw her phone. "I fucking knew it!" she yelled as she paced.

I ran over to her. Grace and I exchanged looks.

"What's going on, Pepper? Calm down."

She put her head into her hands.

"It's Jake, isn't it?" Graces said, taking Pepper's hands and pulling them down.

Her eyes were red as tears chased down her cheeks.

She nodded. "He just broke up with me."

"What, why?"

She shook her head. "I swear I should've seen it coming."

"Did you see it coming, Grace? He was acting weird these last few weeks. Always with a single Hunter and his friends."

"I thought you guys were so tight," I said.

"Fucking asshole. How can he do this to me?"

"He is an asshole, and to do it in a text... what a pussy," Grace added.

"I'm sorry, hun. The good news is there are loads of gorgeous men here tonight. I know you don't want to hear it, but maybe indulge in some mindless sex? That will take your mind off it."

"Yeah." She smiled.

"Or get hopelessly drunk," Grace added.

"I can definitely help you with that. In fact, the bartenders should arrive soon."

"Fuck him, Pepper. You don't need that in your life. Trust me. I ought to know with the number of cheating assholes I've encountered over the years."

She pulled a skimpy dress off the hanger. "Maybe I should wear this," she said, smiling.

"That is gorgeous, Pepper. With your black hair, dark features, and red dress, you'll look like a vixen! Jake will forever regret the message he sent if photos of tonight ever come out."

"Jake, who?" she asked, wiping the tears from her cheek.

"That's the spirit," I said, hugging her.

"Anyway, tell me about Barrett. I've seen in the media about the crane accident this week. How's he holding up?"

I paused. He hadn't really mentioned too much to me about it. He seemed altogether, but maybe there was more to the story he wasn't letting on. Maybe he didn't want to worry me. "It's not ideal, his picture being plastered all over the news, somehow insinuating his company is not adhering to safety guidelines."

"You are the media, Lourde, or your family is. Can't you control it a little?"

"No, and Barrett would never ask me to interfere. I might hold the title of a Diamond heir, but I have nothing to do with the media business. I don't even think Connor or Dad have that level of influence over what gets reported."

"Don't be so naïve, Lourde. The media owns this country."

I scrunched up my brow. "What do you mean? That my family is somehow involved in spreading these lies?"

She put a hand up in the air. "I'm not saying that at all. I'm just saying the media prints what is fed to them, and if it's lies, then that is what gets out to the masses."

"Do you think Barrett leads a dangerous construction company?"

"No, of course, I don't. He's so meticulous with every-thing. He has safety standards above and beyond what regulations require, so I find it hard to believe this has even happened."

"Well, you know what that means, then?"

"No."

"It means someone is out for blood."

"Why would they be after Barrett? He doesn't care for tabloids. He just cares about his business and me."

"His girlfriend, the media heiress." Pepper rolled her eyes.

"True, but we never talk about that stuff, truly."

"Why? Because you're too busy fucking?"

"Possibly." I let my mind wander to the shower this morning and the elevator last night. Heat shot up my spine.

"You slut, you're thinking about his dick again, aren't you?"

"I can't help it," I said, picking up a tube of mascara, and we all laughed.

"I think I'm going to wear this," I said, picking up a canary yellow Yves Saint Laurent dress with a high slit and bustier.

"Very sexy," Grace added.

"Well, it will be now. You're no longer lobster red from your Hamptons sun-baking nap."

"Oh, my God, thank fuck that's over with, and I didn't peel," I added, remembering Barrett's hands on my chest applying the special ointment.

"If you sneak off tonight, we know why!" Grace added.

"As if. Connor is going to be here!"

"Is he?" Pepper shot up a glance.

"Yes, and Ari and Magnus. I invited them all."

"The hunkholes!" Grace exclaimed, using a phrase Pepper coined for the men eight years older than us—arrogant and sinfully good-looking—my brother excluded.

The truth was, Barrett wasn't an asshole at all. Okay, maybe on the surface to get what he wanted, but deep down, he had a heart of gold. Albeit fractured, I hoped I could repair it.

"So you still haven't told Conner yet?" Pepper asked.

"No. I mean, he's got a lot of stuff going on with Dad and the business. I told him I'm working for Barrett."

She shot up her eyebrows. "And how did he take that?"

"He wasn't too bad. He was surprised, but yeah, it was all right."

"How do you think it's going to be when you tell him about Barrett being your orgasm-giver of a boyfriend who happens to also be his best friend?"

"I'm nervous about that. Barrett just wants to go public, though he wants to tell Connor so we can go out and not have to hide our relationship."

"Well, why should you hide?" she joked.

I sucked in a breath.

"You love him, don't you?" Grace added.

"I told him I do, but he didn't say it back. Am I a fool to say that so soon? I feel like a fool when he doesn't say it back." I put my hair in my hands, balling it into fists.

"Hun, you're not a fool. You always put your heart on the line, and that's a noble quality. Maybe he wasn't ready to say it."

I shrugged. "Maybe."

"Has he ever been in love? I don't think I've ever seen Barrett with a girlfriend."

"No, he's never been in a relationship before. Maybe that's why he is apprehensive, or maybe he just doesn't love me." I inhaled sharply, trying to fill my lungs as I breathed in the shallow breaths.

"Oh hun, come on, you're jumping to conclusions," Grace said.

"He declared he wanted to be with you."

"He did kind of suggested we move into together, I guess,"

"Well, holy fuck, why didn't you?"

"Because my family doesn't even know yet!"

"Okay, let's just be patient and not jump to any silly conclusions. Let's enjoy tonight," Grace chimes in.

"Yeah, you're right, you're right. He's done nothing but make me feel special. Maybe he's just not ready. I just can't help but love him. Maybe I should stop saying it."

"You could scare him off. You know what guys are like."

"Okay," I said, scratching my head. Anyway, the party

76

can't start without the party girl slash host. Any minute, we will have caterers and waitstaff arriving, and I'm in my freaking sweats."

"I'm certainly not wearing what I had planned," Pepper said.

"Wear the red dress. It's yours. Be the devil tonight and forget about you."

"Only if you promise me too. Forget about this I-love-you stuff with Barrett.

"Okay," I said, pushing away the nervous thought that there may be another reason why he doesn't love me.

* * *

I walked into the living room and toward the makeshift bar in the corner. Individual bottles of French champagne and cocktails dressed the bar while waitstaff wandered around the crowd of familiar faces with food packaged in cute little takeaway boxes. Friends from school and many social circles filled the ten-thousand-square-foot apartment. Then Grace's cousin, who was here, went and invited a ton of gorgeous men she knew.

My apartment was across two floors, and the party was in full swing with the DJ in the living room, spinning old-school retro and house music.

It was after nine, and I'd already consumed quite a few little bottles of champagne as did Pepper. I'd lost count of how many she had had but by her mood, she was on fucking cloud nine and ready to take home a man and forget about Jake.

I tried messaging Barrett twice already tonight, to which I hadn't received a reply. I couldn't help but be annoyed. This was my housewarming. He was my boyfriend, and out of everyone here tonight, I wanted him to be here to enjoy it with me.

"This view is sensational, Lourde," Grace said, taking in the view of the river from Washington Street.

"I'm certainly not complaining," I respond.

"Oh, it's Dane calling," she said, looking down at her phone.

"Go, take it. I'm going to get another champagne."

I walked inside, where a tall guy I wasn't familiar with walked toward me. "Hey, you must be Lourde."

"That's me!"

"Cool place, I'm Seb. I'm good friends with Gabby."

Gabby, Grace's cousin I was talking about, with the little black book of gorgeous men. And boy, was she right. "Oh, right. Well, hey, enjoy the party," I said, watching his face fall. I walked past him toward the bar when a familiar face caught my attention. "Cool place, sis," Connor said, hugging me.

I looked over his shoulder and saw Ari, Magnus, and Barrett looking wickedly handsome in navy slacks and a black V-neck t-shirt that clung to his tanned biceps. His dark hair swept to the side and begged my fingers to thread through it.

"Hey," I said, trying to sound more sober than I actually was.

"I like what you've done with it. It's better than remaining empty. Moved out and a job in the space of a week. Someone's been busy."

Guilt slashed through my chest, but I willed it away. "Right, yeah. Hey, Magnus, Ari, hey Barrett," I said. And the look he cast my way was dark and devilish, sending a shiver up my spine. *How could we have this insatiable pull over one another after such a short period?*

I cleared my throat. "I'm going to get a drink. Who's

up for some shots?" I asked, wanting to get loose with Barrett and free from the guilt plaguing me about my brother.

Connor grabbed my arm. "You seem different," he said.

My heart pounded in my chest. "Three glasses of champagne, different?" I said offhandedly, trying to throw lightness into the darkness.

"No, it's more than that," he said, his blue eyes serious and questioning.

Shit. I was about to open my mouth and be truthful with him when something behind me diverted his attention.

"Pepper, Grace, how are you?" Connor straightened, and I took a step back and away from his Spanish Inquisition. Thank the Lord for Pepper and that show-stopping dress.

His eyes never left Pepper's dress. I mean, why would they? She looked gorgeous. I looked across and found Magnus and Ari both staring at her and Grace too. Barrett's half-hooded gaze in my direction sent a beeline to my panties.

"Doesn't Pepper look stunning?" I inquired, trying to distract myself from the sex-on-legs in front of my brother and his friends.

"Ravishing, Pepper," Ari said, leaning in and giving her a kiss on both cheeks, followed by Magnus.

"Yes, very nice," Connor said, sounding weird. Was it just the champagne, or was he staring at Pepper way too long?

I turned around to find Pepper staring at Connor. *Gross.* That was my cue to take my leave from any more questions.

"I'm getting a drink. Who's coming with?" I asked, tossing my hair over my shoulder.

"Me," Barrett said, and immediately I felt a shiver when I heard his voice.

"Me too," Ari said, and I wished I hadn't put the offer out there. As much as Ari was cool, I just wanted Barrett all to myself.

I shimmied my way to the bar, moving past the bodies of dancing people.

Barrett was so close behind me I could smell his bergamot scent.

"A champagne for the lady, a Peroni for me, and the old fellow will have a whiskey," Barrett said, ordering on my behalf.

"Hey," Ari said, checking out the gorgeous girls I went to school with who were seated next to us.

Barrett lowered his lips on my ear. "I just want to take you to the bedroom and run my tongue down your seam until you scream my name."

Quickly, I picked up the bubbles and took a long sip before putting it back down in the bar. "I think I'd like that very much."

"Patience, dollface."

He lifted his face back up, and we both turned to find Ari staring at us.

"You two have to tell your brother before he sees what I see. You look like you guys just want to jump each other."

"Shit. How does Ari know?"

"It's so obvious, it's ridiculous," Ari said, sipping his whiskey. "Even the blind can sense your attraction and fucking hormones."

I laughed, but shit, it really wasn't funny. "You're right. Look, tomorrow. Let's just do it tomorrow. I want to enjoy tonight without the drama," I said, toying with the straw in the champagne bottle.

Barrett slid his hand into mine carefully so no one could see and squeezed it.

"Yeah?" he questioned, and I couldn't help feeling what I saw in his eyes. He wanted this. He wanted us. I don't know why I ever doubted him just because he hadn't said three little words.

"Yes," I said, squeezing his hand back. "I don't know why I've waited this long."

"Good, because being a part of this secrecy isn't cool. Now cool your jets till the party is over, so you don't get us all in trouble," Ari said.

"Relax, Ari, Connor won't know a thing."

"Well, by the way Pepper's pulling his attention, you might be right. You sure know how to throw a party, Lourde. The Hamptons and now this? I really love what you've done with the house and in such a short time. We all had dinner together before this, and Connor mentioned you'd only just moved in this week."

"That's true, but I've always known what furniture and style I like, so it was pretty easy."

"And you know shit about interior design, Ari. I don't know why you even say you do."

He laughed. "Is it that different from clothing and couture? That's all about color, textures, balancing moods. My grandmama taught me a lot about her haute couture business."

"Would you ever consider working in fashion?" I asked, surprised to hear about Ari's depth of knowledge on the topic.

"I don't need to work."

"Neither do I, but that hasn't stopped me. This last week was amazing for me. Working has given me more purpose rather than just waking up and wondering what I should do each day."

Barrett looked down at me, giving me a bone-melting gaze that set my heart cocooned in a blanket of warmth.

"Meh, I'm cool," Ari said, checking out some of my model friends who just arrived at the party, then finished the rest of his whiskey before slamming it down on the bar.

"I'm going to think about it now and see if these lovely ladies would like to see Ari's special gift basket."

"Ari!" I squealed.

"Yeah, man, not in front of Lourde."

"You two. So cute." He propped his eyebrow to Barrett and stared at him before sauntering toward the group of tall, lean blondes.

"What was that about?" I asked.

"Ari's attempt at a warning. Nothing for you to worry about, Lourde."

"You make out like me worrying about you is a bad thing, Barrett." I crossed my arms across my chest.

He looked at me, confused. "I worry about this last week you've had and that you haven't really shared any of your hardships with me."

"It doesn't concern you."

"But it does. We're in this together, aren't we?" I asked, an underlying question in my voice. I couldn't help but ask.

"Of course, we are, Lourde. This stuff with the business is just someone out to get me, that's all. I don't want you worrying about that."

"Of course, I'd worry about that. It's normal."

"Would you worry if someone was out to get me?"

"Like the guy that was trying to chat you up when we arrived?"

"What?"

"I saw him. He wanted you, Lourde, he was into you,

and when you walked away, his stare lingered like a fucking hyena to raw meat."

"I... I... are you jealous of him? I don't even know who he was!"

"All I know is you're mine, and I don't want to share you with anyone."

He gave me that hooded stare again, and fuck, what were we even arguing about?

Somehow, he'd pulled me away from my house-warming party, and now my panties were loose around my ankles with his face between my thighs.

"Do you know how hard I am?" He swiped at my clit, and I quivered.

"This is so dangerous," I breathed out, gripping the nearby curtain rods as he delved into my folds. "Ah," I groaned out.

Relentless, he punished me with his tongue, devouring me like he hadn't seen me in days or weeks.

"Oh God, Barrett." I hissed, biting into my cheek and absorbing his assault.

"I've wanted to taste you since you left me this morning, dollface. All I ever think about is you, Lourde," he said, plunging two fingers into me and dragging my wetness to circle my nub.

Heat scaled my collarbone and up my neck. "Fuck, Barrett," I screamed out in muted cries as I shook around him, gripping his head for support.

He buried his face into my folds, pulling another orgasm from me and leaving me breathless.

He got up and was staring at me when I eventually opened my eyes.

I clawed at his belt buckle. But he pulled away. "We've been gone too long," he said, chasing my lips with a kiss.

"Oh, please," I whispered.

"Got you this time, dollface. You don't want to get caught now, do you?" His words were a temptation I contemplated for a moment.

All my relationships had always been in the public eye to scrutinize and splash about. I didn't want that for us. Going public would change that, and I wanted to cling to us for as long as possible. History had shown me nothing lasts forever, but I wanted forever with this man, and it scared me to death.

"No, I don't want to get caught."

"Good girl. Now come on before there are questions about the hostess disappearing at her own housewarming."

10

BARRETT

I was late to her party because Connor dragged me to dinner with the boys. I couldn't exactly refuse, seeing my reason for declining was his sister. Yeah, I don't think he'd take too pleasantly to that news.

Trying to respond to her texts at dinner was difficult, so when I arrived at her party, it took me a nanosecond to spot her beauty—and the guy standing opposite her wanting to fuck her brains out. Okay, so it had me seeing fucking red, even though she did nothing wrong. I was exactly the same seeing her flirt with Finigan at the Diamond family dinner a few weeks ago. Torture didn't even begin to explain the pain that slashed through my chest, having witnessed that fuckery. Now the same feeling was back just from the look that asswipe was giving my girl.

Fuck, get a grip. My moods were shooting from zero to a hundred in a heartbeat. It had to be work messing with me.

News of the fire at 21 Park wasn't ideal, but I was rattled when the crane accident happened this week, and nothing ever rattled me.

I watched Lourde laugh and sip while chatting with

Grace, all the while stealing subtle glances my way. Carefully, of course, because Connor was seated next to me alongside both Ari and Magnus. Oddly quiet, Connor sipped on his whiskey, and I hoped he couldn't smell the delicious scent of his sister's cunt on my lips.

I felt her before I turned round to find Grace and Lourde by the couch.

"Have you guys seen Pepper? I thought wherever she'd gone to, she'd be back by now."

"I saw her a while ago," Ari said.

"Wasn't she talking with you on the balcony, Connor?" Magnus shot Connor a look.

"Before, yes." We all stared at Conner, waiting for more.

"What? She was upset, telling me about how she split from Jake."

"They split?" They appeared so happy in the Hamptons. Why wouldn't Lourde have told me that?

"Yes, they split! What the hell do you care?" Connor's tone took me by surprise. In fact, looking around, all eyes were on Connor now.

I put my hands up in mock surrender. "I don't care, Connor."

Connor glanced away but not before I took note of a vein popping in his neck. Christ, what the fuck was his deal?

Lourde cleared her throat. "We all thought they were solid. Regardless, she's not picking up her phone, she's not here, and I'm worried."

Connor ran a hand through his hair. "I'm sure she's fine, Lourde."

"I wouldn't worry, hun. Pepper always finds her way," Grace added, looking like she'd had one too many champagnes and taking refuge on Lourde's shoulder.

Only a handful of people remained at the party, the ones who were slowly filing out, as final drinks were being served while the handful of others swayed precariously to the cool beats playing from the speaker system.

"Well, this has been fun, sis. I'm glad you're all set up here." It hadn't gone unnoticed that Connor changed the subject. Ari and I exchanged glances, the curiosity in his gaze matched mine.

Lourde sat down next to Grace, who had slumped down beside her and closed her eyes momentarily. "If I'd known living on my own would be this much fun, I would have moved out earlier."

"Have you seen the old ball and chain?" Connor asked, and we all laughed. Grace opened her eyes and sat upright.

"No, not since I've moved out, I've been working." Lourde smiled at me, but behind her seemingly innocent smile held a mischievous look I was all too familiar with. My mind went to all the places we were going to go as soon as everyone left.

Connor slapped me square on the shoulders, dragging me away from imagining bending Lourde over the cool countertop, spread eagle and wet.

"God forbid you would want to walk over to the little company called Diamond Incorporated and help a brother out." He scratched at his forehead, his gaze dropping. Lourde looked from me to her brother.

"I didn't know you needed help, Connor." Her voice was soft, laced with concern.

"I don't need any help." He stood. "Anyway, it's late. I'm going."

"Already?" Ari asked.

"Yes," he snapped.

"Nah." Magnus folded back into the lounge and picked up his beer, taking a sip.

None of us made a move to join him. Why would we? So when the three of us remained seated, he threw us a shaded look, letting out a groan.

"Whatever. See you later." He leaned over, kissed Lourde on the cheek, and walked toward the entrance, leaving the rest of us confused and at a loss for what just happened.

I watched Lourde watch her brother leave. Her arched eyebrows pinched together on her pretty porcelain face. "I hope he's okay." She got up and stepped over Grace to sit beside me, filling the space where Connor had just left.

With the last of the crowd filtering out and Grace curled up on the corner of the lounge, Lourde leaned into me, her hand resting on my thigh. I pulled her closer into my chest, loving the feel of her even more that she wasn't afraid of showing her affection in public.

"So it is true then." Magnus stared at Lourde, then me, his gaze piercing. "I knew it."

Lourde nodded. I'm going to tell Connor tomorrow," she said.

"You are?"

"Uh-huh. I can't keep it a secret any longer." She gazed up at me through her long lashes, and warmth circled my chest.

"Barrett tamed? Who knew?" Magnus shook his head, a grin spreading into his beard.

Even though his life had just imploded with a cheating wife didn't mean he could rain on my fucking rainbow parade. I shot him back a shut-the-fuck-up glare.

"Maybe all he needed was a good woman," Lourde said, squeezing my thigh.

"Evi-fucking-dently," Ari said, taking us both in. I didn't care what either of them thought, and neither did Lourde.

"Just like Dane and me. I think he'll propose soon. I have a feeling." Grace sat up, suddenly coming back to life after a brief nap on the couch.

"Jesus, back from the dead?" Ari asked as we all laughed at the jack-in-the-box that just sprang to life.

"Seriously, oh my God, how exciting, Grace!" Lourde swooned. I wanted to give her that same feeling. I really did, but if I couldn't share my past with her, what future could we really have? One built on lies and mistrust. Losing her wasn't something I was willing to risk.

"What the fuck is going on here?" Connor's voice cut through the speaker bass. Immediately I moved away from Lourde as she disentangled herself from me

I heard Ari mumble something under his breath, but I ignored it.

"Connor, what are you doing back?" Lourde turned around, facing her brother, her high-pitched tone not doing us any favors in the guilty department.

"My jacket."

Fuck.

With my back to Connor, I took in Ari and Magnus. Like two nervous little schoolboys being caught looking through the peephole into the girls' bathrooms, their faces were grim.

"I repeat, what the fuck is going on here. Barrett?"

I slowly stood up, turning around so we were at eye level. I didn't get scared, but the way his eyes narrowed, his nostrils flared, and his shoulder stiffened—in all our years, I'd never seen him look so fucking mad.

"Maybe we should go somewhere more private, Connor."

Connor cross-examined us both, then back around at the lingering people in the apartment who were not so subtly staring our way.

"Fine," he snapped, baring his teeth in barely-there control.

Lourde, who looked like a deer seconds away from being eaten by a lion, was now standing beside me.

"Come with me," Lourde said.

As I walked behind Connor, I noticed Magnus, Ari, and Grace fall in behind us, all following us into the room where Lourde was leading us.

A quick glance back, and I saw Ari shaking his head, Magnus guzzling his beer, and Grace alert and worried for her friend.

Ari grabbed my arm. "We're outside."

Fuck me. I didn't need support. I never had.

I shut the door behind me, feeling the weight in the room and the machine-gun spray of bullets Connor was leveling at my back.

"Tell me what the fuck is going on because I sure as hell don't think my best friend is screwing my baby sister."

I walked over to Lourde so I was standing beside her. She held her hands in front of her, fidgeting with her fingers. "Look, Connor, we wanted to tell you."

"You fucking what?" Connor stepped in to deck me, but I didn't move.

"Stop it, Connor, and just listen, please." Lourde stepped between and caused Connor to step back.

"I love him," she said with her hands on her brother's chest."

"You fucking what?"

"I love him," she repeated.

He looked at his sister, then took me in, in disbelief. Anger mixed with confusion etched his blue now indigo eyes.

"It started in the Hamptons when you suggested I stay with him."

"I knew I couldn't trust you. What did I say to you? I said not to fucking touch her. He is a player, Lourde. We all are. He's slept with most of Manhattan."

"That was in the past, Conner," I said. "Lourde's different. I've never cared about anyone as much as Lourde."

"You fucking asshole!" He leaned over his sister, grabbing me by the shirt.

I lurched forward but did not retaliate when he shoved me with my back against the wall.

"Stop, please, Connor," Lourde pleaded.

"You can fucking hit me, but you won't stop me from seeing her."

His hand smashed into the wall next to my head, but I didn't flinch. Nothing scared me, not even Connor Diamond.

"You can smash my face up, but she means everything to me, Connor."

I stared at him in the eyes, not blinking. His chest rose and fell sharply, and his arm swooped back, ready to strike.

Lourde was behind him, pleading and saying something I couldn't understand.

"Fuck you!" He slammed his fist into the wall, this time piercing through the drywall.

"Do it. I'm a piece of shit, anyway. I don't deserve your sister."

My eyes fell to Lourde, and her fear gave way to confusion. *Yes, dollface, I don't deserve you or happiness for what I've done.*

I exhaled as he gripped his hand with his other hand, almost holding himself back.

The door swung open. Ari and Magnus looked from him to me, then at the hole in the wall next to my head.

"Are you all right, Connor?" Ari asked.

"So you all knew too?" Connor asked, taking the cloth that Lourde passed him to quell the blood dripping from the cuts on his hand.

"I didn't know for sure until I saw them tonight," Magnus said.

"I knew, man, but it wasn't up to me to tell you," Ari said, stepping between Conner and me.

"Is everything all right in here?" Grace asked, taking in the hole in the wall and a shivering Lourde. Fuck, I was so caught up in Connor I hadn't noticed her trembling.

Quickly, I walked over to Lourde, standing behind her and wrapping my arms around her.

Connor's jaw tightened with rage, but he didn't make another move toward me.

"I'm fucking livid," he exclaimed.

"I'm sorry, Connor, we were going to tell you tomorrow."

"He's no good for you, Lourde," Connor said, and I gripped her tighter. The thought of losing Lourde was a stab in the chest, but deep down, I knew he was right. I wasn't good for her. She deserves someone with a clean past, and that's not me.

"Bit looser, Barrett," Lourde whispered to me. "You're squeezing me too tight, Barrett," she said, and immediately, I loosened my grip around her, not realizing I was holding onto her so tightly.

"I think we've had enough revelations for one night, don't you think, Connor?" Ari glared at Connor. *Had I missed something? What was that about?*

Connor narrowed his eyes at Ari, then threw his sister a disappointed scowl. "Does Mom know?"

"No."

"Interesting," Connor said.

"Why is that interesting?" I questioned.

"Because Mom thinks you and Finigan are perfect for one another, so she's invited him to the charity ball in two weeks."

"Oh," Lourde said. "I'll tell her…"

The sound of Finigan's name made my lungs expel air. At dinner, they had something. I could sense it too. That's why it was so damn painful to watch. But fuck, she was with me. She said she loved me. I inhaled, refilling my lungs, and shook away the dagger threatening to plunge into my chest.

"We will tell them. Although I think Dad may already know," Lourde said. "He has a weird sixth sense for this stuff."

"Does he?" I asked

"Fuck this," Connor said. "I can't believe what I'm hearing and seeing. You're eight years younger than him, Lourde."

"I think we all should just go home, regroup with level heads and talk about it when we all calmed down," Magnus said, and, for once, the fuckhead was right.

"First the shit storm with work, and now this? What the fuck, Lourde, seriously?"

"I told you, I'm sorry," Lourde said, stepping out of my grasp and toward her brother.

"I'm out," Connor said, throwing his hands up. "And you, Barrett…" he shook his head, his mouth tight, his jaw set. Then he turned and walked toward the door.

I stared after him, the silence surrounding us bordering on heavy. He was angry, I got that, but it was more than that. He was disappointed and that was the feeling that resonated. I'd let down my best buddy, and that wasn't something I intended to do when he'd done so much for me.

"Lourde just happened, Connor," I said.

He glanced over his shoulder and then walked out.

Magnus and Ari went after him, leaving Grace consoling a distraught Lourde.

I let them have their moment and reflected on the clusterfuck of a mess I'd created because I couldn't keep my dick in my pants and my heart in check.

"I really messed things up, didn't I?" Lourde asked, and Grace pulled her in for another hug.

"It's okay. He will get over it. He's mad now, and that's understandable," Grace said.

Although, mad didn't really sum up the anger that hid behind his eyes.

"I'm happy he knows, Lourde, but I'm sorry you feel like this," I said. "I don't want to see you in pain." But it was too late for that as tears rolled down her cheeks one by one. "I don't want to come between you and your brother. I never want that, Lourde."

11

LOURDE

"You won't. You can't." I pulled away from Grace's embrace and moved into Barrett's open arms. He pulled me close, and I buried myself into his chest. The faint scent of beer mixed with fresh linen lingered, invading my senses and short-circuiting my brain. When I gazed up at him, I found his dark eyes searching mine. I wanted to tell him everything would be okay. Instead, I held my hand to his face, and he leaned in, absorbing my touch, and for a moment, we both let the mess we created dissolve into the background.

"I'll call you tomorrow, Lourde, and Barrett, take care of her." Realizing Grace was still in the room, we peeled away from one another momentarily to say goodbye.

"Of course," he said while pulling me back into his chest. The beating of his heart felt like home. Quicker than normal, it vibrated throughout my body, instantly soothing me.

As Grace walked out, I wrapped my arms around his waist and glanced up. "Do you think Connor will be okay?"

"I don't know. He seemed pretty angry." Barrett stroked my cheek.

It was the truth. I didn't need to ask Barrett what I already knew. I'd never seen my brother that full of rage. Okay, maybe a few times when he and Dad had got into a heated argument, but he had never been that angry with me. We were always so close.

"Even though it's a fuck-stick of a situation, I do feel oddly relieved."

"Because we no longer have to hide."

"Exactly."

"Hiding something can eat you up from the inside until there is nothing else to fester on."

I shifted, glancing up at him through my lashes. His gaze was vacant, empty as he stared into the room at nothing in particular.

"Barrett, are you okay?"

He blinked, his vacant stare no longer there, as he stared lovingly into my eyes.

"I am now." Tucking a strand of hair behind the shell of my ear, Barrett smiled, but it did little to quell the unease forming in the pit of my stomach.

* * *

I woke up to an empty bed. My head hurt from last night, then like a nightmare, I remembered Connor seeing us in each other's arms and the pained expression on his face—it still hurt today. Not long after the argument, we both collapsed from exhaustion in my bed. *But where was Barrett now? Had he left?*

Last night I admitted to my brother I loved Barrett. It didn't go unnoticed that he couldn't say the same about me. But he stood, taking Connor's rage head-on. Unbelievably, he did the opposite of what any man would do when faced with a raging bull with horns that was my brother.

He didn't fight back.

He didn't flinch.

Did he want to get hit?

I stared at the ceiling. Why hadn't Barrett moved out of the way, and why had he said he didn't deserve me? He was the most giving man I'd ever known. He said he was a piece of shit. *Did he really believe that?*

I threw my head into the pillow in frustration. It was as though he wanted to be hit like he welcomed the punishment. But for what? And why did I feel like it was for more than sleeping with me?

He had a dark past, he'd admitted to that, and something was eating him from the inside. All I knew was his sister carried a permanent injury. But what else was there? What wasn't he telling me? And why?

There were too many questions without any answers.

The soft sound of the elevator ding brought me out of my swirling thoughts, and a few moments later, he appeared in the doorframe. Low-slung sweats and a t-shirt that clung to his eight pack of muscles had me doing a double-take. He looked so fuckable standing there, leaning by the doorframe, and like a tidal wave, relief flooded through me knowing he was back.

"Morning, beautiful." He smiled, and it hit its bullseye like an arrow, filling me with butterflies. He took a bottle of water to his lips, drinking the rest of it in one gulp.

I sat upright. "What time is it?" I asked, realizing I'd been lost in the scene of last night and had no clue what time it was.

"It's late, after nine, but I thought I'd let you sleep after last night."

I patted the space next to me, wanting to close the distance between us.

"I smell," he said, pulling at his shirt. "Let me shower first."

"No." I threw the covers off the bed and shot up. "I told you before, I like your smell." After last night, I needed a connection. His mouth on mine, his hands feeling every part of my body like only he can. I needed to know we were in this together.

"Is that so?" His voice was low, his dark eyes not leaving mine as he stalked toward me. Flinging off his shirt, he revealed his toned muscles soaked with the beads of sweat trailing down his chest toward his delicious V.

My lady parts squeezed together at the sight. I traced my hand down the curves of his chest, and he quivered against my touch. "I need you, Barrett," I whispered.

My fingers dropped inside the waistline of his pants. Staring down at me, he held my chin in his hands. "You're like a drug to me, dollface. One hit is never enough."

I moaned at his words, feeling the warmth pool in my belly, and he lowered his mouth on mine in a desperate knee-buckling kiss. With my hands around the nape of his neck, I pulled myself up onto my toes, absorbing his hungry tongue as his thick erection dug into my thigh.

He sucked long and hard on my lower lip, pressing his hand up and underneath the cool satin of my bed shorts. My skin tingled, every sense heightened with his touch. I needed him now.

With both thumbs, I lowered his sweats and underwear enough for him to step out of them.

Breathless, we parted from one another, and his huge cock sprang free. I immediately took him in both hands, stroking him up and down. He groaned audibly, a sound I loved to hear.

After lifting my satin camisole over my head and tossing it to the floor, he took his mouth to my breast, teasing me with his cool tongue. He sucked on my nipple, pulling it as he clamped down. He abruptly released it to switch to the other, scraping his bottom teeth and eliciting all my pleasure senses.

I gripped him firmer, stroking him in a steady rhythm, wanting him to experience the earth-shattering pleasure he was giving me.

He threw his head back momentarily, and I took the opportunity to get on my knees. I wanted to taste him. No, I needed him in my mouth. I slid my tongue over the top, then relaxed my throat, taking him deep.

"Fuck, Lourde," he hissed out, his hands gripping the back of my head. I groaned around his cock, wetness pooling between my thighs. With a burning need, I pulled him deeper, so his thick cock hit the back of my throat, threatening to gag me. The little moans that escaped his lips only urged me further. Fuck, I loved hearing that sound.

"Lourde, stop. I'll blow."

He glided out of me as I glanced up at him through my lashes. "And?"

"And I want to come inside your tight cunt."

Oh.

He guided me up, so I was now standing, his lips smashing onto mine in a bruising kiss. At the same time, he thumbed down my satin shorts to my knees, and I flung them down past my ankles to the ground.

"Turn around," he commanded, dragging his hot gaze across my naked body. "On all fours, dollface."

I did as he asked and shifted back to the edge of the bed, resting on my knees and hands. Anticipation filled my veins, pumping hard throughout my body, waiting for his touch. Finally, his thighs pressed against the backs of my legs, his cock resting in the folds of my ass, and I pushed back into him, desperate for more. Fingers spread me apart —one, then two, and I gasped at the sensation.

"I love how you're so wet for me." His kisses trailed the length of my spine as I arched back into his fingers, causing me to moan.

"Please." I gasped, my lungs burning for oxygen, craving only what he could give me.

He slid his fingers out and groaned. "So sweet."

My pussy ached as I watched him over my shoulder, licking the wetness off his fingers and tasting me.

"You want this, dollface?" With the other hand, he held his cock against my back entrance, dragging it down to my wetness where he had just finger-fucked me.

A guttural sound escaped from the back of my throat, unable to form the words.

"Fuck, I want it too." He filled me with one deep thrust, so hard it pushed me forward. His hands quickly circled my hip holding me back as I balled the sheet into my fist for a grip.

Repeatedly he plunged into me, my tits bouncing from the force, his hands digging further into my hips for support.

"You're everything," he moaned, continuing his relentless thrusting.

"More," I yelled, wanting him to say the words.

He tugged on my ponytail and curled the hair around his hand in a tight but firm grip, my head tilted back. Every nerve ending was lit, and with one deep assault, my pussy spasmed around him in a tsunami of a release.

"Fuck, Lourde," he said as his cock throbbed, and he shot me full of his seed.

With my arms like lead and legs like jelly, he let my hair

go, causing my head to hang low as I tried to claim back my vanishing breath. His hand wrapped around my stomach in a bear hug from behind. He didn't let me go, and I placed my hand around his, feeling the warmth of his embrace.

Before he pulled out, he placed a kiss on my mid-back. I immediately collapsed on the bed and rolled over onto my back.

A grin spread into his cheeks as he leaned down to kiss me on the mouth. Yeah, there were no words.

"Can I shower now, Ms. Diamond?" he eventually asked.

"Now you can shower." I laughed.

"Then I want to take you out." He smiled, not just with his mouth, but his eyes shone like two emeralds. Light and love spread onto his face, and I don't think I'd ever seen Barrett happier than in this moment.

We were going out in public together for the first time.

"Let me make a call first, but I'd love that."

He side-eyed me. "Of course."

I smiled.

"Why don't we just visit your parents now?" he asked.

What? "Really?"

"Absolutely." He grinned, then stepped into my shower, leaving me on the bed with a more- than-satisfied vah-jay-jay and a full heart.

Barrett turned the shower on, and a stream of water followed. I rolled over, spotted my phone on the bedside table, and sucked in a huge breath.

What would Mom think? She'd planned every boyfriend I'd ever had, making sure they came from a respected family and were, of course, rich.

Barrett had success, ridiculous success, but he was new money as Mom would say. He didn't come from a prestigious family and had a past he didn't want to divulge.

I shook away the feeling he was keeping something from me and decided to call Dad instead of Mom.

"Lourde. How's the apartment?"

"It's great." I paused. "Are you and Mom home?"

"Yes, dear. Why?" He sounded concerned.

"I was going to come round shortly, that's all."

"Splendid. Shall I ask the chefs to organize lunch?"

My heart beat erratically. I had a strong suspicion Dad knew about Barrett when I'd spent the weekend at his place after the dinner with Finigan.

"Yes, please, for me and one other."

He paused before adding, "Sure."

"Thanks, Dad, see you soon."

* * *

Barrett glided us through the streets in his McLaren. Only, it didn't last long with Manhattan traffic—even on a Sunday. We came to a stand-still around the corner from Park Avenue.

Having a car in Manhattan was crazy. Barrett knew that, but it didn't stop him from buying more than one. Taking them out from time to time, he said he loved the feeling of freedom it gave him.

I remained cautiously optimistic about our lunch, but I was nervous if my bouncing knee was anything to go by. He reached over the center console and put his hand in mine.

"It will be fine." His perfect mouth tipped upward into a bone-melting smile.

"Do you think so?"

"I do," he said, inching the car forward, so we were only moments away.

"How are you not nervous?"

He shrugged. "Who said I'm not?"

"You are?"

"It's not every day I go to my girlfriend's parents' house."

"Well, at least you know them!" I said.

"I know they want their daughter to be with someone respectable and someone from a good family."

He stared at the cars ahead, the silence lingering between us.

I squeezed his hand. "You are respected, Barrett. And once they know you mean everything to me, they will be happy. Shocked but happy. Anyway, I think Dad already knows."

"Alfred's not the one I'm concerned about."

I stared out the window. "I know."

Mom was the one who wanted me to marry a son from a blue-blooded family. Heck, she'd try royalty if she could but settled for politicians. Finigan was the perfect choice, being the son of Governor Connelly of Massachusetts.

Neither of us said anything more. When we arrived, Barrett parked, and we got out. In the elevator, he took my hand in his, the gesture comforting.

"Showtime," he said as the doors pinged open into the penthouse.

12

BARRETT

Jesus, fuck, I was more nervous than a politician at a rally.

Knowing Alfred and Elizabeth for years did little to curtail the bubble of sweat forming on my brow. I had lost count of how many weekly dinners I'd had here. In the early days when Connor wanted to know about my family—and I divulged that they died in a car accident and my only sister lived in Boston—he'd opened his home to me. The invitation had remained when he'd moved out of the family home and into his own.

If they knew my past involved such a newsworthy headline, one that could risk the Diamond name, I doubt we would be associated in any way.

"Hello, Lourde, Mr. Black, what a surprise to see you today." Dressed in perfect black and whites, Gretchen, their longtime housemaid, greeted us as we stepped out of the elevator. It only took a second for her to notice my hand wrapped around Lourde's.

"Hi, Gretchen," we both said at the same time, followed by a giggle from Lourde.

The edges of Gretchen's mouth turned upward. Clearing her throat, she signaled us inside. "Mr. and Mrs. Diamond are in the dining room."

"Thank you, Gretchen," I said, leading the way like I had so many times before. But this was different, very different.

Lourde squeezed my hand as we walked into the penthouse foyer, past the living room, and stopped just before the dining room doors.

She turned to me, panic flaring in her hazel eyes. "My stomach is in my throat."

Tilting her chin up and grazing her lips with a quick kiss, my fingers lingered along her jaw. "I've got you, dollface."

Nerves bounced around in the pit of my stomach, and it was a strange sensation to be faced with. Million-dollar deals were nothing compared to this. Uncommon and definitely not what I expected, the nerves ping-ponged like they had some kind of control over me. I stared into Lourde's eyes, and the nerves pushed into the crevices of my stomach so I could focus on only her.

She lifted her hand to mine. "I've never been happier than when I'm you, Barrett."

I kissed her forehead and breathed in her heavenly calming scent.

Perhaps I wasn't such a monster after all. The way she looked at me through innocent eyes made me think marriage, kids, a puppy, and a white picket fence were possible with Lourde by my side.

Marriage? I just imagined that, didn't I? Fuck me.

If she believed in me, then why couldn't I be the man she needed me to be, not just for a minute but a lifetime?

I opened the double sliding doors. Elizabeth sat at one

end of the dining table scrolling on her phone and Alfred at the end closest to us, reading the paper.

Elizabeth glanced across the large marble table at Lourde, then me. "Barrett?" she questioned before rising to stand. Her gaze fell to our intertwined hands, blinking a few times, her brows creased into a line. "Right. Oh… okay."

"Elizabeth. Alfred." We both walked inside as Alfred turned.

I watched as Lourde left my grasp and kissed her father first, then her mother on the cheek. Then I followed behind her, greeting Elizabeth with a kiss on the cheek as well.

She tilted her head, examining her daughter's choice in men—not her own—in a lingering gaze she hadn't leveled at me before today. She took her hands to her temples, massaging them in round circles. Over the years, I noticed she did that when she was uncomfortable. Well, that made two of us.

Slightly uncomfortable, I turned to Alfred and shook his extended hand. "Nice to see you, Barrett, although I had a feeling you might be joining us today."

"Likewise, Alfred."

His grip was tighter than usual, his stare clear as a summer's day—*take care of my daughter, Barrett*—his handshake conveyed, and I shook it firmly with my response—*Lourde is the world to me, I fucking love her. I'd die for your daughter.*

He blinked, and at that moment, there was a gentleman's understanding.

"So, let's sit, shall we? Looks like we have much to discuss." Alfred signaled for us to sit at the two seats beside him, and I pulled the chair out for Lourde.

So far, so good. I cast my gaze toward Lourde, checking in to see if she was okay.

"Mom, I love your hair. Did you do something different?"

Okay, so she was still slightly on edge and trying to butter up her mother, knowing flattering her always worked like a charm.

"Yes, Francesco decided a change was needed with the ball coming up, so he cut it and baylaged it."

I put my hand on hers at the table in a reassuring gesture, and her mother's gaze fell to our hands.

"So I'm very surprised," Elizabeth said, taking her seat at the end of the table.

"I know, Mom."

"How long have you two been together?" she asked.

Lourde turned to me. "We started seeing each other in the Hamptons." I decided to keep it vague.

"When she was staying with you, Barrett?"

"Yes, after she found Hunter cheating."

"Never liked that jerk, Hunter," Alfred said.

"He came from a family of—"

I inhaled sharply. Was Elizabeth more interested in setting her daughter up with a proper family than for love?

Lourde quickly interrupted. "He cheated on me, Mom."

Their chef set salads in front of each of us. Before he retreated, he smiled at Lourde and me.

Lourde and I thanked him while Elizabeth and Alfred exchanged scathing looks. I wondered if Lourde had noticed the not-so-sweet exchange between the powerful couple at opposite ends of the table.

Alfred picked up his fork. "Well, I'm happy for you both."

"You're the same age as Connor, aren't you, Barrett?" Elizabeth asked, and it was a fair enough question, one I knew she knew the answer to. The truth was, the age gap had never come into question when Lourde and I were together.

"I am, Elizabeth."

"Lourde has always been an old soul. Age gap aside, I think you're perfect for each other."

Lourde squeezed my hand, and I exhaled, not realizing I was holding my breath. "Thanks, Dad."

"I guess so. Just not what I was expecting, dear. I am a little blind-sided, that's all. Barrett's already part of the family."

"Thanks, Elizabeth," I said but stopped short of eating as everyone else had. "I want you both to know that Lourde means everything to me. She is a beautiful woman, inside and out, and I promise to be the best man I can be for her."

The room went silent, and for a moment, I replayed what I had said, thinking I may have said something wrong.

I glanced around the table. Lourde stared up at me, a slow smile forming as my words sunk in while Alfred had a tender expression, and Elizabeth smiled.

"That's very sweet, Barrett," Elizabeth said, dipping into her salad.

Lunch went perfectly. Actually, it really couldn't have gone much better. It was easy once we got the elephant in the room out of the way. Plus, there was the added bonus that I knew her parents well enough, it was just another meal shared like all the dinners we'd had before.

Alfred leaned forward so only I could hear him. "A word, Barrett?"

Okay. That had my fucking nerves shooting all over the goddamn place.

"Sure."

I slid my hand away from Lourdes and slid out of my chair. She stopped mid-conversation with her mother about the various charity auction items up for grabs at the Diamond Charity Ball this year, then looked from her already-standing father then to me.

"Scotch time." I smiled, reassuring her.

"At one o'clock?" She curled an eyebrow in disbelief.

"Just a quick one," Alfred said. "Don't worry. You won't even know he's gone."

Her father patted her on the shoulders, and I tossed her a smile, despite the nerves settled in the pit of my stomach.

I had nothing to be nervous about. They'd both been pleasantly surprised at lunch. Alfred even seemed happy for Lourde. *So, nerves, take a back seat, would you?* I walked into the den like I had hundreds of times before after dinner with Connor.

Alfred walked over to the liquor stand, removed the lid to the crystal decanter, and poured two scotches.

I took it from him and waited till he sat down on the leather armchair before following suit.

"Cheers, son."

Son.

He held out his glass, and I held up mine as we met halfway and clinked in a toast.

"To Lourde."

"To Lourde," I echoed his sentiment as I took a sip of the amber liquid.

"Don't fuck it up, Barrett."

I nearly choked, quickly swallowing it down before it came out. "Noted."

"She always liked you. You'd have to be fucking blind to miss that."

"Well, truth be told, I think there was always something there. We just couldn't do anything because of Connor."

"Connor. Ha! Shit, does he know? I can't believe I forgot about him."

"We told him last night at Lourde's housewarming party."

"I see. How did that fair?"

"Pretty badly, actually. Lourde didn't mean to hurt him."

"He'll get over it."

"Is he okay?" I asked, noticing a change in my friend over the last few months since he stepped up at the Diamond Incorporated company.

"I don't know. I wish he would just commit to something. Sometimes I wonder where I went wrong with him." Alfred took a sip of his scotch and stared vacantly across the room.

"Surely you don't mean that?"

"Absolutely, I do." He held my gaze before shaking away whatever thoughts were going through his head.

"So I was just reading about you before you arrived or rather, your trainwreck of a week."

"You of all people should know not to believe everything that's printed." I widened my eyes, and he shot me a piercing glare.

"Shit, too far?"

Then he split into laughter. "I think you should be more concerned about your reputation at the moment and fixing this mess up you've got yourself into than what is printed out there."

"I know you print what your reporters find, but honestly, Alfred, I think someone's out to get me."

He put his tumbler of amber liquid and leaned in. "How so?"

"I've run this business, taking it from the ground up, employing hundreds of people over the last decade, and in the last two weeks, my award-winning tower at 21 Park has a fire with the cause of suspected arson." I paused, running my hand through my hair. "Then less than a week later, the crane braiding cable snaps."

I shook my head.

"But who would put people's lives on the line like that?"

"Someone's out to get me."

"Why? What are you hiding?"

I diverted my gaze at him, and he looked at me curiously. Hiding that my parents didn't die in a car accident, hiding that I held the gun that killed my mother because I couldn't fight off my father. And that my father shot himself in the head in front of my sister Evelyn and me.

No. That was something I could never divulge to anyone.

"You're a businessman, Alfred. Not everything we do is entirely by the book, is it?"

He tilted his head and let out a chuckle.

"There's always a sprinkle of gray in there. Always has to be when you become as successful as we are."

"I can't prove it, but I think I've pissed off the board members at the Hamptons deal that's just gone through."

"Ah yes, you mentioned something about that. What happened?"

"I know I can trust you, Alfred, so I will tell you this in confidence. The board was misappropriating funds while fucking around and laying off staff. So I did what any ruthless businessman would do with that piece of information. I asked for a hefty discount in the acquisition in order to keep their dirty secrets."

He threw his head back in laughter. "So a little black-mail. No one fairs well to blackmail."

I knocked back the rest of my scotch. "I'll sort it out. I have my team on it."

"Do sort it out because now you're with my daughter, and we can't have any smudges against her name." His previous lighthearted tone had changed to a serious timber tone.

I blinked. He just said the obvious, so why was I surprised. "I know."

"Good, so get your ducks in a row, Barrett, if you are as serious as I think you are with Lourde. Otherwise, this won't end well." He stood up, putting an end to the conversation.

The fucking relic was threatening me. Anyone else would be on the goddamn floor for doing such a thing. But Alfred was Lourde's father, and I respected him. Still, I didn't take to threats well.

That side of him that Connor always talked about had reared its head, and it was ruthless.

13

LOURDE

I t was like someone had lifted a weight off my shoulders, and I felt fucking free. Freer than ever before. And by the carefree boyish expression on Barrett's face, he felt it too. I squeezed his hand on my thigh, watching him paddle shift gears and glide along Park Avenue, but instead of taking a right to my place, he kept going straight.

Elated, the news was finally out, and we didn't have to hide from anyone, it took me a while to register we had veered off course. "Where are we going?" I asked.

"I think we should celebrate, don't you?" His hand trailed up my thigh, his fingers skirting the fabric of my thong.

"What did you have in mind?" I breathed out in a whisper of a breath.

"I want to take you away for the night."

"Now?" I gazed up at him in surprise, and his grin appeared wider on his golden-colored complexion.

"I have nothing with me, and tomorrow morning, I have a meeting with the kitchen contractors."

"Olivia can handle it. Anyway, I'll have you back by ten." His fingers toyed with the lace of my thong. My skin tingled and popped with goosebumps, and it took me a minute to remember what we were talking about.

"Are you sure?" I asked, not giving two fucks about any kitchen contractors whatsoever at this point.

"Positive. My housekeeper will organize clothes and everything else you need so you can just relax."

"What if I don't want to relax?" A husky voice escaped me.

His finger dipped underneath the lace, his finger rubbing over my fold.

"Barrett." I breathed. "I don't want to crash."

He laughed like I was crazy, but fuck me, if his fingers kept circling my nub like that, I was about to explode on his leather seat.

"I want to fuck you into the night, Lourde."

"I'd like that," I said, crossing my legs and absorbing every moment of his touch. The lights turned red and fuck, thank God for tinted windows because he was nipping and sucking at my neck and collarbone while finger-fucking me hard.

He groaned out. "You're always so wet for me, dollface."

A tent peeked in his pants, and I imagined licking and stroking him with my tongue.

I closed my eyes, feeling the roar of the engine and the pull into the seat as we sped away. My thighs tensed, and I groaned out as he filled me again, dragging my wetness to my nub as I clenched around him.

Opening my eyes, I turned to find him grinning.

"You are one wicked man, Barrett Black."

"Never said I wasn't." His grin wavered momentarily before he returned his gaze to the road.

I pulled my dress back down, and when I looked up, we were downtown, pulling into the heliport.

"Oh, are we going to the Hamptons?"

"Yes, we are. What better way to celebrate than where it all began?"

I was ecstatic. Could this day get any better?

He opened the door for me, and I stepped out. "After you, Ms. Diamond," he said, planting a kiss on my lips and swatting my ass.

I turned to him, wrapped my arms around his neck, and didn't care who saw us. Brushing my lips across his, I kissed him as he pulled me into his chest.

He groaned out. "I think this helicopter ride will be torture, knowing I can't spread your legs and hear you scream my name."

I bit down on my lip, the familiar ache between my legs responding to his dirty words. "Well, what is it they say? Absence makes the heart grow fonder, right?"

"It's not absence if I have to look at you across from the chopper now, is it?" Half-hooded eyes trailed my body from head to toe, then back up at me.

"Come now, I'm sure you don't want to make the front page of the news with public indecency."

"I wouldn't give a fuck if it was with you." He squeezed my ass, and I let out a yelp.

"Barrett!" I tsked out, but he was right. I couldn't wait for his hands all over my body too. This chopper ride couldn't go quick enough.

We walked past the entry, and Barrett greeted the staff at the heliport. A woman dressed in a maroon and white suit behind the counter stared from Barrett to me, trying miserably to conceal her surprise at the sight of us. "Everything is ready for you, Mr. Black," she said, signaling us through the double-glazed security doors.

"Thank you," he said, and we walked out onto the tarmac holding hands.

As far as helicopters go, this one was very nice. Okay, so I wasn't actually referring to the Sikorsky S-76 but rather how Barrett dragged his fingers into my folds while we were flying over the Long Island Sound and gave me fucking orgasm after orgasm. But believing in delayed gratification, he wouldn't let me return the favor.

As the helicopter was preparing to land, I turned to him. Something had been on my mind since lunch. "Are you going to tell me what Dad said when he took you into the den?"

"You're a clever girl, Lourde. Take a guess."

"Hmm." I tapped my fingers on my chin. "Something like Lourde is my only daughter, take care of her, she's my princess…"

"Something like that." Tilting his head down, his gaze met mine. "You might always be his princess, but you will always have my entire fucking heart, Lourde." My ribcage squeezed as the air escaped from my lungs, leaving me speechless and out of breath.

The engine cut out, and immediately, I unclipped my seat belt, too worked up to be seated. I climbed onto Barrett's lap, wrapped my hands around the nape of his neck, and kissed him with my entire heart.

"What did I do to deserve that?" he asked, his hand feathering my jaw.

"Just being you."

The pilot cleared his throat. "Excuse me, Mr. Black. We have arrived."

He laughed, and I let out a giggle.

"It seems we have. Thanks, Jordie."

The side door opened, and a stewardess spun her

moment of surprise into a pleasant, well-rehearsed smile. "Mr. Black, Ms. Diamond, welcome to the Hamptons."

* * *

It was after three when we arrived at his oceanfront Hamptons house. Only a few weeks ago, I left here in a tangle of knots after he'd pushed me away. I walked out past the pool to the balcony, the summer afternoon breeze whisking my hair off my shoulders and tossing my lilac dress about.

"You know, you never took a swim with me when you stayed here." He appeared behind me, his voice soothing like a warm hug.

I turned to face him, the sunlight turning his eye color to sea-green sage. "No time like the present, then?" I said, tossing him a wink. "But, I don't have a bathing suit."

"You don't need one." His gaze circumnavigated my body like Christopher Columbus, sending the hairs on the back of my neck to attention.

I bit my lip. Slowly I unbuttoned my dress, his hooded eyes not leaving mine. It dropped, along with my thong, pooling around my ankles. Next was my lace bra. Unclasping it, I tossed it to the ground.

Sheltered under the foliage of trees, I knew his house was Fort Knox when it came to privacy, and with the recent upgrade in security, my privacy was the last thing on my mind as I stood there in my birthday suit.

"Your turn, handsome." I stepped out of my dress and took to unbuttoning his pants while he unbuttoned his crisp blue shirt.

He lowered his mouth to one breast, then the next, tugging on my nipple with his mouth and sending a lifeline to my groin.

He stepped out of his pants and briefs, then peeled off his shirt, revealing a sculpted athletic body.

"Come with me," he said, taking my hand and leading me down the steps into the pool.

Deliciously heated, the warm water soothed my skin as I glided throughout the clear water. A delicate splash made me turn. Swimming the length of the lap pool, Barrett's strokes were gracious, his body athletic like the twisted man of steel he was.

I swam over to the corner where he stood, watching him toss his hair back, the motion suspending water through the air.

"It's gorgeous in here." Scissoring my legs around his hips, I felt the warmth radiating from his skin.

He gripped both my ass cheeks with his large hands. "Ever come in a pool, dollface?"

Thickness lined my throat as my breath evaded me. *No. Never, but I fucking want to.* My teeth dragged across my bottom lip in anticipation.

He shot up an eyebrow, then spun me around—my back against the pool coping. Kissing me hard on the mouth, I groaned into him, wanting all of him.

I yanked at his hair, tipping his head back and kissing his neck, sucking on his skin.

With his thick and full erection, he thrust into me, and the feeling was… words escaped me momentarily at the sensations wracking over me.

Cold, hot, and full, so full.

He groaned, and my nails dug into his back. "Fuck, Barrett," I purred. "That feels…" I pulled him closer, and he pressed me harder against the wall. My legs around his hips pressed him into me.

"Tell me you love me, Lourde." He breathed out, and my gaze fell to him.

"I love you, Barrett," I said, and my heart expanded.

He stopped mid-thrust. His chest, rising and falling. He was breathless, but it was more than that. He was struggling for air.

My heart beat erratically as he scanned my face. Behind his eyes was fear. He wanted to say something, it was there behind his eyes. I ran my hand up to his cheekbone.

"Do you love me?" I blew out on a whisper, my heart in my throat.

He nodded. "I do. Fuck, I love you, Lourde." His face was a mixture of strain then relief, and he took his lips to mine. Our tongues intertwined in desire, undying desperation, and fullness only he could bring me.

"Show me," I said. "Show me how much you fucking love me, Barrett." My gaze fixed on his, he thrust into me, our eyes never leaving each other.

His breath grew shallow as did mine.

I groaned loudly, my body hot. The water swished around us as Barrett quickened his strokes. My legs tightened around his waist, and as I stared deep into his eyes, I lost all control. We came together with an intensity almost too much to take.

14

BARRETT

Right before I said those three little words, my world stopped. Inside her, on the edge of the pool, my head spun. Nausea flipped my stomach in two, but I couldn't wait any longer. And what better time to tell her than when she stared into my goddamn soul, stealing the breath from my lungs.

We made love again two more times that evening, and everything was right in the world. I could die tonight and be the happiest man on the planet because of Lourde. Okay, well, maybe that wasn't true. I'd be the happiest man on earth, then I'd be fucking pissed knowing Lourde and I were ripped apart, and I was in heaven—or hell.

But she made that hole in my heart disappear. She was the the healer of my wounds, the light to my dark soul.

Don't fuck it up.

Don't fuck it up

Don't fuck it up.

"What are you thinking about?" She stroked the few hairs on my chest around her finger.

"Nothing."

"Doesn't look like it."

I trailed my gaze toward her, hovering over her swollen lips from earlier kisses.

"I'm just thinking about something Alfred said."

"I knew you weren't telling me something. Dad is a big scary man, but he is a soft teddy bear on the inside."

"Ha! Sure he is," I added.

"What did he say?" She propped her head on her hands, waiting for me to answer.

"Just to get my ducks in a row."

"What ducks?"

"Work and whoever is after me."

"What does he care about ZF Construction?" I watched her bow-shaped lips twist into a frown. "Oh."

"You're everything to him, Lourde. But you should know your family avoids drama like the plague, and if this gets out of hand…" I rubbed my temples, feeling a headache coming on.

"It won't," she said. "You're a respectable and ethical businessman, Barrett. Dad knows that." Still, I couldn't help the doubt that lingered.

"It still doesn't change the fact that my company is under attack. The fire and crane accidents aren't random events. Alfred's concern is reasonable. You're lucky you have him looking out for you."

She pulled my face close to hers. "Hey, come on." She scanned my face, looking for more, but I wouldn't let her see it. I couldn't. My love for her made me selfish.

"I'm fine, Lourde," I said, taking her hand in mine and kissing her knuckles. "Anyway, tell me about the townhouses in Brooklyn."

I was thankful we moved off that topic, and for the last half hour, she spoke about how much she'd enjoyed her first week working with Olivia on the project. My hand stroked her back as her head nestled onto my bare chest. Not long after, her breathing slowed, and I knew she was asleep.

But as she snored lightly, her breath a warm dusting of air on my forearm, I wondered if love conquered all, and, if so, could she look beyond my dark past to be with me forever?

* * *

Work was a perfect storm of meeting after meeting with department heads. When I informed my assistant, Aimee, I was arriving after ten, I could hear her gasp down the line in surprise. *Shock, horror, the boss is coming in late.*

News of Lourde and I was out. Ari had texted me photos of Lourde and me at the heliport splashed about in *USA today* and *BuzzFeed*, and I had to tell Ari to stop sending me the images. Fuck, the media was lightning fast, but with the general public carrying iPhones, making a quick buck had everyone chasing down anyone, and privacy was at an all-time low.

Fuck it, I didn't give a fuck who knew and why. All I knew was Lourde and I were in our own little bubble of happiness, and nothing or no one could ruin that. Not even my last meeting of the day with my security duo and media director.

"Right, well, there's no guessing what's on the agenda." I took my seat, drinking the triple espresso in front of me in one swoop. Placing it down, I caught sight of Ivy, my media Director.

"Barrett, don't you think I should have known about Lourde? I'm already dealing with a boatload of media requests about the fire and the crane accident. Now, this?" Dark circles appeared below Ivy's blue eyes, her foundation cracking at the corners of her eyes and mouth. Ever since ZF Construction caught the media's attention— which was after the completion of my first boutique hotel in Soho— Ivy had been on my team, but on this occasion, she wasn't happy.

"It's no one's business but ours, Ivy."

Ivy looked from me to Barton, who glared back at her. Don't expect anything from Barton, Ivy. The man was a tall glass of metal and arctic ice. That's why I hired him.

"Are you suggesting we make no comment or statement?" She lowered her gaze back to me.

I flicked through the dossier Barton and Jesse had prepared for me. Pictures of the crane accident site were enlarged and showed the damage of the snapped cable. This was more important and what I needed to focus on.

"How do you want me to handle this? I mean, Ms. Diamond is well known. She's basically royalty in this country. We can't stay mute on the matter with these photos of you two kissing at the helipad!"

I put the important dossier down, leveling her with one look. "Let me make this crystal clear so there is zero confusion, Ivy. There will be no comment on my relationship in the public eye."

"But Barrett, that is impossible with…" She held her hands out, clearly exasperated.

I held my hand up, cutting her off. "It is definitely possible. I make the rules, and where Lourde is concerned, we are strictly private. No comment."

I held my gaze like fire on hers.

"Okay," she said, shaking her head.

"Now onto the real issues at hand. Where are we at with the investigation into the crane accident?" I looked at Barton then to Jesse.

"The video surveillance on-site was conveniently

blacked out at the time. But they didn't count on the footage from across the road." Jesse grinned.

"What did you find?"

"It's pixelated, but I'm working on cleaning it up," he said.

"Work faster. I want to catch whoever is trying to fuck me over and bury the asshole. Anything on the fire?"

"Nothing. Whoever lit that covered their tracks or is paying off someone high up," Barton said.

"Fuck!" I slammed my fist on the table. "I know they're connected."

"We will find whoever did this, Barrett. You know we will. We just need more time," Barton added, a steely determination in his eyes.

"I know you will. I just hope it's sooner rather than later." Alfred's words swirled in my mind, and my heart hammered away. I wouldn't lose Lourde to some lying-fucking-asshole trying to screw me over. I was Barrett-fuck-ing-Black. I came from nothing and turned my life around. I ate fuckhead's like this for breakfast, lunch, and goddamn supper.

"At least the press has put that story on the back burner. Pictures of you and Lourde together are getting mid-six figures," Ivy added.

"And they say the Kardashians made it rich quick. What the fuck is this world coming to, seriously?"

"I hear you, but people love a fairy-tale story with a fairy-tale ending." She smiled, and I got the feeling she was happy for me.

I laughed. "Is there any such thing?"

She leveled her gaze at mine. "Only you know the answer to that." Happily married, Ivy was as far from your closet romantic as they come.

And just perhaps, I felt like happily ever afters existed for even the mere monsters among us.

"Well, if that's it," I said.

"There is something else," Jesse said.

"What?"

"Jessica, Olivia's assistant, just disappeared. She has seriously gone off the grid. She hasn't used any form of payments in weeks. Her credit cards and bank accounts have not been touched. We've had someone watch her apartment in the Bronx, and she hasn't been back since she disappeared.

"What the fuck?"

"We also followed up with her employment contract to track down her emergency contact, but when we searched for it, it wasn't there," Barton added.

I had a sinking feeling in my stomach. "Do you think she's involved with whatever that is going on here?"

She was quiet but good at her job. Apart from that, I didn't know too much about her, and I didn't care to. But Olivia said she was okay.

"We're looking at everything. Nothing is off the table, sir," Jesse said, folding his arms on his chest.

"We need to find her. I want more resources on this. I don't care how much it costs. No one fucks with my company and my people."

"I've got a crew I know can help with more resources," Barton suggested.

"Good. Get it done. I have to go," I said, checking my watch and making sure I could leave on time to meet up with Lourde. She was due back at the office any minute, and I didn't want her waiting another second.

I walked back into my office, where she was already waiting.

"Rough day?" she asked, walking toward me in her tight black skirt that hugged her delicious curves.

"I'm good now that I've seen you."

"I see." She took her lips to mine, and I devoured them in a hungry kiss.

"That bad?" She stepped back, not expecting my assault on her lips.

"Let's get out of here," I said, pulling her hand.

15

LOURDE

Somehow half the week had rolled past, and it was now Thursday. The new owners of the townhouses were moving in tomorrow, and we had so much to do between now and then.

I finished shopping at a new designer I suggested for the foyer vignettes, buying unique pieces to complement the cabinetry and furniture. Shopping on a budget, although very healthy, was something new, and shopping with a time restraint, I found to be challenging—a positive one—and I achieved it. Well, for the most part.

"Thank you, Ms. Diamond, for the business." Genevieve, the owner, had appeared after I purchased half the store, dressed in a plaid jacket and purple pants suit. She was just as cutting edge as her luxury items.

"Pleasure. These pieces aren't for me, personally, but rather, a luxury multi-townhome development in Brooklyn by the award-winning construction company, ZF."

"Really?"

"Absolutely, all eight of them. Perhaps there could be

the possibility of a collaboration in the future if you're open to that?"

"Are you kidding? I mean, of course." She cleared her throat and opened a drawer to her desk. "Here's my card. Call me, and we can discuss it over lunch."

"Perfect."

"Boys," she signaled for her carriers. "Ms. Diamond is ready."

"Thank you." I smiled and walked out to the van where Jeremiah, my driver, waited.

Waiting for nearly two hours inside, Jeremiah quickly jumped out as he saw me exit the store with bags and the men behind me.

"Lourde, let me take that." Jeremiah took the parcels from my hand then assisted the men with the other items, loading them into the van.

"Thanks, Jer."

Before heading back, I wanted to get the team some sustenance. I noticed the little shop a few doors down. The sweet baking smell called to my attention.

"Jer, would you mind finishing loading? I'll be back in ten minutes," I said.

"Of course."

Pastries of all types stared at me from the glass counter. I'd purchased most of the items, knowing how hard everyone had been working and likely had not had time to stop for lunch.

Then I ordered ten coffees, ranging from lattes to macchiato. I didn't know what everyone drank except Olivia. She lived on espresso, easily three times a day.

I handed over my black Amex and waited, taking in my surroundings, full tables, idle conversations, and not-so-subtle glances.

People stared. That wasn't new, but there were definitely more stares since news broke that Barrett and I were together.

I quickly stepped outside just to break from the stares and whispers, almost crashing into a chest.

"Sorry!" I said, sidestepping the oncoming person.

"Lourde?"

"Finigan... hi."

He leaned over and kissed me on the cheek, my skin heating under his touch.

Dressed in an open white shirt with the sleeves rolled up and tan suit pants, he looked decidedly handsome. "So, did we ever stand a chance?" he asked, raising an eyebrow.

Oh, shit, the photos.

"I don't know," I said, looking down. "Perhaps if Barrett and I weren't together, yes," I said, and it was probably the truth. *Why was I getting all flustered?*

At the dinner, Finigan and I got along. Sure Barrett had been sitting opposite, and I was trying to make him jealous as hell, but it turns out, in the process, Finigan was an all-right stand-up guy and good-looking.

He held my arm. "Hey, it's okay. Barrett's one lucky guy."

"Thanks." I smiled, feeling relieved. "Hey, and for what it's worth, I'm sorry. I didn't mean to hurt you or mislead anyone."

"I know, Lourde. You're one of those rare special breeds that have a heart. Not like all the sharks out there."

"Sharks?"

"Yes, they either want you for something, or there's always an agenda. And with my dad as the governor of Massachusetts, women want me."

"And you're complaining?"

"I've had enough of that to last me a lifetime. Is it wrong to want to settle down?"

Oh.

"It's not wrong at all. I hope you find your ever after, Finigan."

"Thanks, but I think she may already be gone."

I blushed from ear to ear. "That's not true," I said in a low tone. "You're handsome, kind, and intelligent."

He grinned. "Am I?"

Shit, now I was flirting. "Yes, well, I'm sure you know all of that."

"Lourde."

I'd never been so relieved to hear my name called.

"Hey, my order's ready," I said, flustered.

"Clearly it is." He stared at me, and my heart rate quickened.

"I'll see you," I said, breaking the stare.

"You will, at your family's upcoming ball. I look forward to it."

"You're coming to that?"

"Of course."

Of course. My family invited the richest, most prominent families in and out of town.

"Okay, see you there."

"I look forward to it, Lourde."

"Yes. Me… okay. Bye," I said, waving my hand in a flustered flap.

* * *

"I brought snacks," I said in a loud voice, returning with pastries, coffees, and cakes for Olivia and the rest of the team working around the clock to get the houses finished.

As if on cue, everyone stopped what they were doing and swarmed toward me.

"Oh, you fucking gem," Olivia said, taking the brown

paper bag from my hands and distributing the sweets around.

"Coffees too," I said, placing the carrier down so everyone could help themselves to the much-needed stimulant.

"How did it go?" she asked, looking at Jer, who placed a box down in the loading area.

"All done," I said. "Got the throws and cushions, and the vignettes for the entranceway are sorted."

"And all within the budget?"

"Well, I may have gone over slightly, but you should see what I have planned."

"You haven't disappointed me yet." She opened the containers and pulled out a melted ham and cheese crois- sant. When she took a bite, her face morphed into one of pure ecstasy.

"Oh, hell yes," she said. "Everyone out, no eating on the wood floors."

The rest of the team went outside into the backyard. A few of them had been staring at me, and personally, I just wanted to get on with the job, not become more tabloid gossip for the contractors.

"Do you mind if we go out front?"

She looked up from me to the two women in particular who had been gossiping. "Good idea."

I sat on the steps leading to the front door, and Olivia sat down next to me. "You okay?"

"Yes, fine." She looked at me. Olivia had suspected we were an item as soon as she had seen Barrett and me together, but I hadn't confirmed it since the tabloids hit, nor had she brought it up.

"Okay, maybe that's a lie." I took a sip of my coffee. "I've always been in the public eye, but this is different. The gossip and stares have upped to another level of creepy, if I'm honest."

"Honey, they're just jealous, is all. Barrett is a catch, and, of course, you are too. Put the two of you together, and it's like Kate and Will. But I'm guessing you're both not that proper behind closed doors." She wiped the flakes of pastry off her mouth and split into a grin.

"Olivia!" I elbowed her.

If you only knew.

"Look, I'm not used to what you obviously get, but I know one thing. Don't let it come between you and Barrett. I've known him for a very long time, and I've never, ever seen him this happy before."

"Really?"

She gripped my wrist. "Truly."

"We love each other, Olivia," I admitted, knowing she was more a friend than a boss.

"Well, no shit. I could tell that the moment I saw the two of you together."

I laughed. "Were we that obvious?"

"To me because I know him so well, yes, absolutely."

"Do you know much about his sister, Evelyn?"

"Only that she lives in Boston. She has some kind of permanent leg injury. Barrett tries to get there when he can, but he hasn't been in a while, come to think of it."

"Hasn't he told you this?"

"Yes, no, I knew that."

"Do you know about his parents?" I asked, trying not to sound too much like a creeper but wanting to know what Barrett had told her.

"Only that they died in a car accident when he was a kid. It's tragic, really."

"Yes, I couldn't imagine that, growing up with just my brother and without my folks. It would certainly harden you up very quickly, having to fend for yourself."

"Hey, look on the bright side, he found you, and you, him. Let the other stuff float away like the shit-eating dust gossiper it is, and enjoy it. It's a very rare thing indeed."

Something banged and crashed inside, and I instantly jerked to get up.

"Fuck! What is it now?" Olivia said, placing a hand on my shoulder and pushing me back down. "Finish your coffee. You haven't stopped working, Lourde. I've got this."

"Thanks, Olivia. Hey, what are you doing Saturday next week?"

"Probably drinking a bottle of red and watching *Notting Hill*. Why?"

"Oh, I love that movie. How about you come to the annual Diamond Charity Ball? I'd love you to meet my friends, Grace and Pepper. I think you'd love them."

"Sounds fancy."

"It is, very."

"Well, all right then." She winked.

"Well, all right then," I echoed.

16

BARRETT

Walking into the completed townhouse after the tour, I was impressed. *Wow.* Olivia and Lourde had pulled a rabbit out of a hat and not only completed the townhomes in time for the new owners tonight, but they blew it out of the park. They even made the award-winning design at 21 Park look modest in comparison.

"I rarely get surprised, but this is something else," I said, admiring the display on top of the featured round table.

"Oh, thank fuck," Olivia said, relieved. "That was all your girl there," she said, pointing to the console.

I laughed. "I wasn't that much of a ball breaker, was I? Actually, don't answer that. Did you do this?" I asked Lourde.

She nodded. "Do you think the new owners will like it?" Oblivious to her own skill and natural abilities to style a room, she stood there waiting for an answer.

"Absolutely," Olivia and I both said in unison.

She bounced up on her toes and smiled. "I'm so glad you think so."

I smiled back at her. From an heiress without a voice to a woman with drive, an irrefutable talent. My heart constricted in my chest just seeing her claim her true potential, and it was all her doing.

"Yeah, okay, so I'm going to go now before I die of exhaustion."

Lourde laughed.

"Girl, I don't know how you're still standing, but thank you from the bottom of my heart. You did good," Olivia said, pulling her in for a hug.

Why hadn't I seen it before? They were alike in so many ways. Of course, they'd strike up a friendship.

"I have so much to learn. Thanks for showing me the ropes, Olivia."

She let go of Lourde and turned toward me. "She's sure as fuck got my vote to stay on. Jessica who?"

I let out a laugh as she referred to the absence of her second-in-charge, who was still missing.

"Noted, but that's up to Lourde, not me," I said.

"Thank you. I'm humbled," Lourde said.

She stopped short of committing to a job, and I wasn't sure how I felt about it.

Olivia threw me a curly eyebrow then turned back to Lourde. "Well, if I don't see you next week, I need your help picking me something to wear for the ball and not something that costs ten-K. We aren't all born as Diamonds!"

"Of course!" Lourde said, splitting into laughter.

"You're coming to the Diamond Charity Ball?" I asked.

"Yes, your lover invited me." I threw her glare. "Lourde invited me, Barrett. Relax."

"I think Olivia would love Pepper and Grace, don't you?"

I shook my head. "How do I know?"

They both laughed.

"Well, I'm done. Going to pass out now," Olivia said.

"Well, great job as always, Olivia, and Lourde, I'm seriously impressed. And here you thought you lacked the skills."

"You did?" Olivia turned to her.

Lourde shrugged.

"Crazy girl," Olivia said, grabbing her briefcase.

"Right, let's go. The new owners will be here any minute, and I don't want to get stuck talking to them."

"You know, for someone so successful, Barrett, you are so private," Olivia said.

"That's the way I like it."

I put my hand into Lourdes, so proud of my girl. Squeezing her close, she cautiously glanced up at me, and I gave her a reassuring smile. I didn't care that Olivia saw us together. I was fucking beaming.

* * *

Lourde washed up after cooking us both a delicious dinner. It was completely unnecessary since I had a housekeeper, but she shooed me away to my den to tend to some urgent emails that just came through.

An hour later, I went looking for her but couldn't find her.

After checking the kitchen and living room, I rounded the corner and opened the door to my bedroom. There, she lay in bed, still clothed from the day. I walked over to where she lay, eyes closed, her chestnut hair splayed across the pillow, her alabaster skin showing a faint blush on the tops of her cheeks.

"Hey, I must have nodded off," she said, leaning up and propping herself up on her elbows.

"You've been working too hard."

She shook her head. "Did you get your work done?"

"Uh-huh." I pushed her hair away.

"So you really think I have a talent for design?" she asked.

"I do."

I dragged my thumb across her mouth, her warm skin dancing like fire on mine.

"So, your two weeks are up…"

"Are you going to fire me?" She purred, and my dick twitched in my pants.

"Why, have you been bad?"

"I spent more than I should have today on the company Amex."

I shook my head and clucked my tongue in a disapproving *tsk*. "That's a definite no-no, isn't it?"

She nodded. "I think it is," she whispered, so her breath fell on my cheek.

A tingle shot up my spine. "In that case, I ought to fire you…"

"Oh no, please, isn't there some other way?" She dragged her nail from my lips, down the column of my chest, resting on the button of my suit pants. "I think you should punish me another way."

"Is that so?"

"I think you should punish me, hard," she said, cupping my balls through my suit pants.

Fuck, I love this girl.

"I think you're right."

She dragged her teeth across her bottom lip, and with love-drunk eyes, she unzipped her skirt while I ripped apart her blouse, sending buttons ricocheting across the floor. Her eyes flared, and I marveled at the beauty before me wearing nothing but a plum-colored lace thong and matching bra.

I roughly chased her mouth with a kiss and inched her back onto the bed while I undressed, careful not to get my hard dick stuck in my zipper.

Fuck, I'd missed her, every inch of her skin. I dragged her legs apart and nipped her skin, taking it between my top and bottom teeth, tracing the inside of her knee up to her thigh.

"Wait here," I said, reaching underneath the bed to quickly unwrap a package.

Her eyes lit up like saucers. "Oh," she breathed out. "That's big."

I held up a black vibrator I'd been wanting to try on her. "You can take big, can't you, dollface?"

She nodded and kissed me hard, her teeth digging into my lip and sucking it back into her greedy mouth.

With a flick of my thumb, I turned the vibrator on and sank it into her wet pussy. Over and over, I dipped it into her tight cunt, watching her squirm and writhe until she came in a fit of waves around it.

"We're just getting started."

She moaned and folded up, swiping her tongue across my tip.

I shuddered, craving more of her.

"I'm sorry I spent more, *boss*. How can I ever make it up to you?"

She liked role-playing, the little minx. Well, I'd give her an Oscar-worthy performance she'd never forget.

"Get on your knees."

She grinned but did as I asked.

"Now you're going to take everything I give you."

She dragged her hand down to her pussy and rubbed herself while taking me in her mouth.

"Who said you could pleasure yourself?"

I pushed her hand away, and she groaned, taking my cock deeper.

I hissed out. Fuck, her warm, wet, and magical tongue was enough to tip me over. I gripped the back of her head and pushed into her hard and rough until she gagged.

"Ah, fuck," I said, quickly pulling out.

"Why did you do that?" She looked at me through her lashes, her lips deliciously moist.

"I don't want to come inside your mouth. I want to explode inside your tight little cunt."

With one quick and fast pull, I yanked her off the floor and into my chest, kissing her as our tongues thrashed about in a war of wanting.

"Turn around. I'm going to fuck you so hard you'll be begging me to stop."

She threw me a wink then turned around. "The harder, the better," she breathed out.

I spanked her ass so hard she jerked, then clamped her knees together, savoring the after sting. I bit her ass cheek, and she howled like a fucking wolf, the sound making me harder than a steel rod.

With her pert ass in the air, I reached for the vibrator and dragged it over her asshole.

"I want to fuck both holes, dollface."

She groaned and pushed back, so the tip of the vibrator went deeper into her ass.

"You want this too, don't you?" I went in another inch, then back out again.

"Fuck yes," she breathed out in a whimper.

Without waiting, I dipped the vibrator inside of her, inch by inch as she let out a gasp.

"You're a naughty fucking girl. I hope you've learned your lesson."

Repeatedly, I sunk the vibrator inside her back-hole, watching her scream with ecstasy. But I couldn't hold out anymore. With my other hand, I gripped onto her ass, plunging into her sweet pussy.

"Fuck, Lourde," I said, taking her deeper and harder while continuing my assault on her ass.

I felt her on the edge. Moaning louder than ever as she gripped the sheets, I plunged into her, digging my hand into her hip bones.

"Barrett," she moaned as she spasmed around me, and my cock quivered inside of her. Slowly, I inched the vibrator out—teasing and lengthening her orgasm.

"Holy hell." She purred.

"Don't think you'll go over budget again, will you?"

"I think I will!" she said through gritted teeth, falling onto her back and trying to catch her breath.

17

LOURDE

I woke up Saturday morning in Barrett's bed with a rose beside me and a note.

Gone for a run… minx x

Memories of last night came flooding in. Holy hell, a vibrator… and in *there*. I didn't think life could get any better—mind-blowing sex for starters and a man who was truly and utterly amazing, who loved me for me.

He'd given me a lifeline, an escape from the clutches of the Diamond name. He'd given me the confidence to move out, not give up on my dream to work and carve out a purpose that I never could as a Diamond woman—working wasn't something my mother and grandmother ever did. Supporting husbands and the family and organizing social events that had Manhattan's finest flocking was what they did, but that was not enough for me.

I pulled the flower to my nose—the velvety dusty pink petals brushed against my skin while the sweet fragrance filled my nostrils. Throwing the sheets off, I leaped out of bed and strode out of the bedroom. Never had I ever felt so complete.

While preparing two yogurt and granola bowls for breakfast and waiting for Barrett to return, I decided to call Pepper. Maybe this time, she'd actually pick up my call.

"Hey, Pepper, finally!"

"Oh, hey."

She sounded off. "You all right? Where have you been? I've tried calling."

"Yes, I know, sorry. I just had the flu, so lying low."

"Since when?"

"I think all that boozing at your party hit me over the head the next day."

"So you've been to Soho? I thought you might go back to the Hamptons and get your things after you know what happened with Jake."

She laughed. "Hell, no. I organized a carrier to send them back home."

"Do you need me to come by and make you some soup or something?"

"No!" she yelled out.

"*Okay,* I know you're stubborn, but geez."

"Thanks, hun, but I'll be fine."

"Hey, by the way, what happened to you at the party? You just disappeared."

"Oh, did I?"

"Yes, Grace and I were worried."

She laughed, but there was a nervousness to her laugh I couldn't ignore.

"Did you get lucky, Pepper Little?"

"Okay, fine. Don't ask me his name because I couldn't tell you I was that drunk."

"Oh, hell to Jake then!"

"Jake, who?" she teased out, and we both laughed.

"Well, you best get better because next weekend is the ball, and there will be some gorgeous men there."

"Oh, I wouldn't miss the annual ball for anything!"

"Speaking of the ball, Finigan is going."

"Finigan, the man your mother set you up with a few weeks ago, Finigan?"

"How many other Finigan's do we know, Pepper?"

"True. And how do you know he will be there?" she asked in an accusatory tone.

"I bumped into him the other day in Brooklyn."

"Interesting, and how did he react to the news of you and Barrett?"

"He asked if we ever stood a chance."

"Oh, bless him."

"And he said he thinks I'm a rare and special breed."

"That's sweet apart from the animal reference."

"Pepper, come on! It was kind of sweet, actually."

"Wait, do you like him, Lourde?"

"Of course not. I'm in love with Barrett."

"Uh-huh."

"Oh, and he's in love with me," I added, the smirk on my face unfolding naturally.

"He said it?" she shrieked down the line.

"He said it, Pepper!"

"Oh, hun, I'm so happy for you."

A noise sounded in the background, then the phone was muffled. "Hey, I'll call you later."

"Pepper?"

"Byeee!"

That was strange. Her phone must be acting up, I thought, as I placed the berries on top of the yogurt and drizzled it in maple syrup—okay, drowned.

The sound of the elevator doors was perfect timing. As I turned, Barrett strolled toward me in the kitchen. His gray shirt darkened where sweat attached to his wall of muscles.

"Morning, dollface." He pecked me on the cheek.

"Morning, handsome."

"I'd say I would shower, but I think you like a sweaty man."

"You know I do, plus the yogurt bowls are ready."

"Perfect."

"So what does a construction company tycoon do on the weekend?"

"Work, usually."

"Oh." I stuck my chin out, hoping to spend as much time with him as possible.

Sensing my disappointment, he rested his hand on mine. "What did you have in mind?"

"Hmm." I tossed a blueberry in my mouth, and an idea popped into my head.

"Fancy being a tourist for the day?"

He laughed. "I've never been a tourist in this city before."

"Sure you have." I elbowed him in the ribs as we sat side by side.

"Truly. I haven't. Never had the time."

"You're telling me you haven't been up the Empire State Building, Coney Island, taken the ferry to the Statue of Liberty?"

He widened his eyes. "Nope, never had time, Lourde. And had no one to do it with."

Damn, how can he make my heart flutter just like that?

"Well, be prepared, Mr. Black, because I'm your tour guide today."

* * *

He pulled his hands tighter around me as his head nuzzled into the curve of my neck.

"I can't believe you've never been up here, Barrett," I said, nudging his scruff with my cheek.

"Do you know how many times I've driven past the Empire State building?"

"Countless?"

"Countless. Yet, I've never bothered to stop or ever thought to take the elevator to the 102nd floor. It is a pretty view from up here," he said, looking at the horizon. The sun lowered, turning the blue sky into a canvas of lilac and warm tangerines.

"Thank you for today." He planted a soft kiss on my cheek.

"You're so welcome." The day of sightseeing started by taking the ferry to Liberty Island to show him the Statue of Liberty up close and personal. From there, we hopped over to Ellis Island, then Coney Island. Then we popped into the MET museum to actually admire the art rather than just attending an event which we both had done. Now my legs were like lead from all the walking and sightseeing.

"Although you've definitely let me see another side of you."

I turned to face him. "How so?"

"Who knew bumper cars would turn you into a possessed Daytona driver."

I laughed and hit him on the chest with my fists. "Hey, I can't help it if you were in the way."

"You T-boned me!"

"Only because you were in the way." I grinned and wrapped my arms around his waist.

"I did lie about one thing," he said.

"Oh?"

"Grand Central Terminal, I'd been there before. Actually, loads of times."

"Why didn't you tell me?"

"Because I'd never been there with you."

"Oh."

"Before moving to Manhattan permanently, I'd take the train from Boston to Manhattan every morning and evening, but I barely looked up at the beautiful ceiling. I never had time. Always rushing to appointments or getting back in time to be with Evelyn for one of her many operations."

I held my hand up to his face. "That must have been a hard time," I said, wanting him to open up to me. There was more to his childhood than the abuse. I was sure of it.

"It was. It still is, if I'm honest. That's why I haven't told you everything. My past is buried. It's just too painful."

"Maybe you should talk about it. It might help you, Barrett."

He hadn't said no, and ten minutes later, we were back in his apartment where he was sweating bullets. His control and confidence had vanished and was replaced by a shadow of a man I wanted to hold and protect from whatever demons he was facing.

"Barrett, I understand if it's too hard to talk about. I'm sorry, I shouldn't have pushed you."

His hand slid out of my grasp, and he paced the floors of his living room.

"It is, but I have to tell you. I love you, Lourde, and that means no secrets."

I swallowed down the lump in my throat.

"I'm a monster." He stopped and searched my face, waiting for a reaction.

Tempted to correct him, I did nothing but choose to remain silent so he could continue.

"My parents didn't die in a car accident like I told you and your family."

Oh, God. Did he murder them? What the hell, Lourde, as if?

"O-okay." I breathed out on a stutter.

"Ever since I could remember, I grew up in an abusive household where my father took pleasure in hitting us. You know that part but what you don't know is he forced himself on my mother many times. I can still hear her screams in my nightmares."

"Oh Barrett…"

"Let me finish. Otherwise, I don't think I can get this out."

I nodded.

"I'm scared I'll lose you if I don't tell you everything, but I'm terrified you may never look at me the same again, Lourde."

"Barrett, I love you. Nothing can come between that." Nerves crawled up my back and spine, settling in my chest.

He stared at me, fear clouding his eyes.

"That fateful day, I'd had enough. I knew where Dad stashed his Smith and Wesson revolver, and while he beat Mom and my sister in the kitchen, I escaped, running to get it. I wanted to kill him, Lourde. I wanted him to die for what he'd done to Mom and my sister."

"Barrett." I gasped.

"The monster took a cup of boiling water and threw it on her just because he could."

"Oh, my God. If he did that to her, what did he do to you?" I croaked out in a weak whisper.

"Whatever you can imagine."

I got up and walked over to him, but he took a step back.

"I was his punching bag, Lourde, his ashtray, a mistake from a rape encounter with Mom resulting in a pregnancy.

It was Mom who fought to keep me when he wanted me aborted."

The backs of my eyes pricked with tears.

"I returned with the gun and wanted to pull the trigger but couldn't. As much as I wanted to, I couldn't take a life." He shook his head. "The next thing I knew, he was on me wrestling me to the ground."

He looked away, bringing his hand to his forehead, his green eyes, pools of agony.

"During the struggle, the gun went off, hitting my sister in the leg and causing permanent nerve damage."

"The operations…"

"Yes, many surgeries to try and repair the damage. Again, I tried to wrestle the gun, but he was too strong. As I watched my sister fall in agony, the gun went off again. This time, hitting my mom square in the chest."

"No," I whispered as tears flowed down my cheek.

I walked over to him, taking his hand in my own and forcing him to look at me.

"Barrett, this is not your fault."

"I held the gun, Lourde. If it weren't for me, that gun would never have been there in the first place."

"You can't say that. You were only trying to protect your mom and Evelyn."

"Instead, I turned out to be the monster who killed my own sweet mother."

"No, Barrett. Your father killed her. You were just a kid."

"He pressed the trigger, but I wasn't strong enough to stop him. I wasn't strong enough to protect the ones I loved the most. And it's because of me she is lying in the ground at a Providence cemetery. It's because of me, Evelyn lives with a permanent disability."

His eyes glassed over, and he looked away. He'd been

living with this regret and remorse for nearly twenty years, and he needed to see he wasn't to blame in this tragedy.

"It's because of you she's free from him. They both are."

He jerked violently.

"What is it? Wait, how did he die, Barrett?"

"I ran toward Mom's lifeless body, blood pooling around her as she took her final breath. That's when I looked up, and he had the gun, pointing it from me then to Evelyn. That's when I charged at him. I had nothing to live for. I wanted him to kill me. He took the very person who mattered the most to me, and I wanted him to rid me of my pain. But instead, he turned the gun on himself, shooting himself in front of us both."

Tears fell steadily, and my body shivered. I leaped over to him and wrapped my hands around him, pulling him down to me. "Oh, Barrett."

"I don't deserve you, Lourde."

"Shh," I said, holding back sobs.

"I'm a mon—"

"You are a hero. You're not a monster. At sixteen, you had the courage to confront your father and protect your family. How could you ever think I would think of you like that?"

"I don't know." He hung his head.

"I'm so sorry you had to go through this and carry the guilt with you every day. But you need to know it's not your fault... none of it is. You were only trying to save your mother, but things turned out the way they did. You couldn't predict it, nor could you fight a grown man."

"But I wish things were different. I wish she was here. I wish she could meet you, Lourde."

"I wish that too, Barrett, but the last thing your mother

would have wanted for you is to live a life carrying this guilt."

He squeezed me tighter then took his mouth to mine in a soft, tender kiss.

After a beat, we parted, and I took him in. Strain crossed his face but also relief.

"Come with me," I said and held his hand as we strolled toward the bedroom.

Fully clothed, we folded into bed, and after only a few minutes, his breathing slowed, his eyes closed as he fell asleep on my chest, exhausted. I held him, replaying everything he'd told me, and another tear fell from the corner of my eye.

He wasn't a monster. He could never ever be a monster. But he was the one who had to believe that, not me.

18

BARRETT

Sunday morning came around, and when I opened my eyes, for the first time since I could remember, I didn't have that weight of dread in the pit of my stomach.

Lourde slept soundly beside me. Light snores escaped her as she breathed against my arm. Laying in the clothes we wore yesterday, everything about last night came flooding in like a warm bath.

She hadn't thought I was a monster, had thought nothing of the sort. Her teary response caused my breath to hitch in my throat. I'd expected her to flee, not stay.

For once, I couldn't help but think about my happiness, and the possibilities were endless with her. I wanted her so much it hurt. I wanted to be with her night and day, day and night. I wanted to wake up with her every damn day and make love to her every night. If my dreams were any indication of what I wanted, we were already there.

After we'd eaten, showered, and made love, Lourde had suggested we go visit Connor—unannounced, of course. Connor had ignored her calls all week, and she'd had enough of the silent treatment. They were close. I got that. That was a common denominator we shared as I did with my sister, so I understood when she said she wanted to clear the air with her brother.

* * *

"So, have you considered what you want to do now you've finished up your two weeks?"

"Somewhat, I guess."

"And? You know you can do whatever you want, Lourde. You can probably start your own design company."

She laughed. Did she doubt her own abilities?

"I'm not kidding. I can see talent. That's mainly my job. People think I've gotten to where I am by myself. It's not the case. I recognize talent in people and employ them to work around me. Otherwise, we wouldn't have this company valued at a billion dollars. So you could just say I'm a recruitment specialist," I said, punching in the code to Connor's private garage.

"You're a bit more than that. And anyway, Olivia is the one who's super talented."

"She is, and I recognized that. That's why I pay her very well."

"Not well enough to buy a ten-K dress, apparently!"

I turned to Lourde, confused. "That's untrue. Her last bonus was upwards of a few hundred grand."

"Really? What does she do with her money then?"

I shrugged, pressing the accelerator, and we glided forward into the parking bay. "Who knows. Anyway, you're avoiding my question."

"I am?" Her question came out on a purr.

"Lourde."

"Okay. Look, I haven't decided what I want to do. All I know is that I loved the last two weeks and want more of that."

"Sounds like you have decided then."

"But don't you think it's weird me working for you?"

"Why?"

"Well, for starters, the women give me dirty looks when I come to the office."

"What women?"

She rolled her eyes. "Seriously, Barrett?"

"I'll fire them."

"You can't do that!"

"I can do whatever I want."

She rolled her eyes again.

"Tell me what you want, Lourde. Whatever it is, it's yours."

"Well, I want to work with Olivia, but I don't want any special favors. I want to work my way up."

I glanced over at her, and she gave me a steely glare back. "You're serious?"

"As a bullet."

"No special favors."

"And a normal salary for someone with my skill set."

"Lourde, come on."

She folded her arms. "Then, no deal."

"What?"

"You heard me. I want to be treated like everyone else."

"But you're anything but."

"I don't care. For once, I want to earn something. I want to prove to myself and others that I'm capable without my last name carrying me through."

"Others won't think that, though you know that as long

as you work for me, they will see you getting special favors."

"As long as you, me, and Olivia know that's not the case, then I'm fine with that."

"Well, fuck, I wasn't expecting that," I said, pulling into the parking spot and killing the engine.

"I always like to keep you on your toes, Barrett."

"You do, that's for sure," I said, unclipping her belt and lifting her over the center console.

She let out a yelp but giggled in my arms as they came to rest around my neck.

"Does that mean I won't be getting any lunchtime specials?" I grinned and took her lower lip in mine, then released it after nipping it.

"I'm sure we could come to some understanding there." She grinned and ground her ass against my crotch.

"Hmm, why wait till then?"

"Because we are in my brother's parking garage!" she said, kissing me chastely on the lips then releasing the door handle.

I groaned out, adjusting myself.

"Come with me, handsome." She extended her arm and tried pulling me out.

I laughed at her lame attempt. "Okay, Mr. Two-Hundred-Pounds of Twisted Steel and Sex Appeal!" she said, and I split into roaring laughter.

"Oh yeah, that's me, absolutely."

"Come on, before I change my mind, and we really give the tabloids something to print about."

"Coming," I said, slapping her ass.

We walked up to the door and pressed the buzzer, looking into the video screen.

It rang and rang.

"Maybe he's not home?"

"He's home," she huffed out.

She rang it again. This time, he picked up.

"Who's there?"

"Connor, it's me."

"Lourde?"

"Yes, who else! Barrett's with me. Can you let us up?"

"Barrett's with you?"

"Yes, now let us up, weirdo."

"It's not a good time, guys."

"Ah, we won't be long, Connor. Now, could you just get over yourself and stop being rude?"

"Fuck, fine."

The buzzer sounded, and she pushed the gate, leading us to his private elevator.

"He sounded weird," she said.

"Yeah, he did. Maybe he's still weirded out about us. His best friend and sister, come on, you have to feel for him a little."

"Since when are you the sensitive type?"

"Since you softened my angles to curves, Lourde."

She smiled, agaze with unblinking awe. I was only speaking the truth, and fuck, it was so liberating.

"Some things you come out with should be printed on a Hallmark card."

"Well, if construction fails, I'll definitely keep that in mind."

She squeezed my hand and kissed me on the cheek. The doors pinged open, and I pulled her close to me.

Connor met us at the elevator doors. "What are you doing here?" Adopting a hard smile, he stood at the entrance, blocking our entry.

"Well, hello to you too, brother." She let go of my hand and placed two hands on the tips of his shoulders, pecking him on the cheek.

She stood back and glanced at him. "Did you just get up?"

"No." He ran a hand through his wayward hair. "I've been working."

"Hey," I said, extending my arm in a peace offering. Apprehensively, he shook it, then let it go.

"Hello, Barrett," he said with poison on his tongue.

"What can I do for you both? Like I said, I'm busy."

"Well, that's no way to treat us now," Lourde tsked.

"Said by my sister, who was screwing my best friend behind my back?"

She put her hands on her hips, and her ass moved deliciously. Okay, now wasn't the time to think about all the delicious things I could do to her peachy ass.

"We were going to tell you, Connor. I'm sorry you found out the way you did, but you are just going to have to accept we're not going anywhere. I love him, and Barrett loves me. Let's just try to be adults about this."

Connor looked from his sister to me as we loitered in the foyer like strangers.

"Look, Connor, for what it's worth, I'm sorry. I didn't want you to find out like that. We had no intention of this happening. It just happened."

He let out a nod and a sigh. "Yeah, tell me about it."

Wondering if we were still talking about us, I glanced at Lourde, who shrugged, then pushed past him into the living room.

"Where on earth is your housekeeper?"

We followed her into the main living area with a view to the kitchen, where dishes stacked high in the sink. Come to think of it, I don't think I'd ever seen his place so unkept. There were clothes on the floor, hanging off furniture and stuff everywhere.

Lourde picked up some of the clothing on the floor

instead of stepping on it. "It's like a tripping-hazard in here."

"Is everything all right, Barrett?" I asked him quietly— this was so out of character for him.

"Yes, I'm fine. I'm just busy, and my housekeeper has the flu."

"So does Pepper," Lourde said, overhearing our conversation with the hearing of a bat. "Must be going around."

He ran a hand through his hair, and was that a bead of sweat bubbling on his brow?

"Must be. Now I've got a mountain of files to review before the board meeting tomorrow, so I think you guys should leave."

"Leave? We just got here!" Lourde said, ignoring him and making her way into the kitchen. "At least let me have a quick espresso."

Connor looked at me, and I shrugged. There was no point arguing with her, and he knew that.

"Make it quick. You know where everything is, Lourde."

"Well, Jesus, not through this mountain of plates and glassware. It's like you had a party here or something." She clattered around, opening cupboards. "Do you guys want one?"

"Yes," we said in unison.

"Thanks, Lourde," I added.

"So, is Alfred busting your balls again?" I asked, taking a seat in his tan chesterfield lounge.

"Always." I waited for him to continue, but he didn't. He just sat on the edge of the seat, looking very uncomfortable.

"Usually, I'm vague as fuck, not you."

The sound of the coffee machine cut through our exchange.

"I'm just busy doing board stuff, you know? So tell me, what's happening with you? Any closer to finding out who's after you and determined to ruin you?"

"Getting there. But are we seriously going to talk about this right now, or are we going to address the beef between us?"

"What can I do? You fucked my sister. I can either punch you out or accept it."

"Okay, for starters, you know you couldn't punch me out. I've got at least twenty pounds of muscle on you."

He let out a laugh. "It's not about brawn, and I'd call it ten even."

"I know I'm not what you and your mom wanted for her. I'm not old money. But we're happy. I promise you, she means the goddamn world to me, and I'd do anything to protect her. I love her, Connor. She knows me, she knows everything about me, and she accepts me for who I am. She doesn't want to change me. She loves me. Do you know how rare that is for guys like us?"

Lourde placed two coffees in front of us. "Thanks, hun."

"You guys are the real deal, aren't you?" Connor questioned, looking at me, to his sister, and back to me.

"I'm all in when it comes to your sister."

She gave me a heart-melting smile. "Me too."

Connor took his espresso to his mouth, an expression of resignation appearing on his face. "Well, then, fuck it, I can't stop you."

I looked at Lourde, and her expression mirrored mine. "Are you serious?" she asked.

"Yeah, you're not talking out your ass, are you?" I

asked, completely taken aback from his complete one-eighty.

"I'm serious. Just don't fuck it up."

Lourde's grin curled upward into her cheeks. I was equally confused but happy because I knew how much it meant to her to have Connor accept us.

"I didn't think you'd be this cool," she said, walking around the coffee table and giving her brother an enormous hug. "Thank you, we've always been close, but this means the world to me," she said, releasing him then skipping off toward the kitchen to fetch her own cup of coffee.

"Truth be told, I really don't think you would have stayed away from him if I hadn't given you my blessing."

"Probably not," she said over her shoulder.

She walked back and sat on the seat opposite. "It means the world to me that you can find it in your heart to be happy for us, Connor," she said, taking her cup to her lips.

A thud down the hallway pulled our attention.

"What was that?" Lourde asked.

Connor stood up. "Nothing. I've just got the window open. Anyway, I'm glad you guys are happy, and we shared this moment, and it's been great, but I really have to get back to work. Alfred wants me to follow up then and present tomorrow being Monday with the board, so I'd really appreciate it if we might organize a lunch this week, or I'll see you at the ball on Saturday."

I finished the rest of my espresso, uncertain if Lourde noticed the sense of panic lacing Connor's words. "Sure thing, buddy."

Lourde looked over her shoulder as we walked to the elevator. "Is someone here?"

Ha, she did.

"No." He pressed the elevator call button eight or nine times, repeatedly.

There was someone here, I was sure of it, but I wasn't going to be a dick about it because Lourde would want to know exactly who it was, and he just said he gave us his blessing. I didn't want to rock the boat.

"Is there?" Lorde asked. "Who is she?"

"No one." The doors opened, and he pushed his sister back into the elevator. "I'll see you on Saturday. Be good to her." He held his finger up at me with a steely glare.

"Always," I said.

"And you be good to whoever is in there." Lourde let out a giggle, and Connor's lips tipped into a smile.

"I'm working now. Would you just go already!"

"Bye, brother, love you."

"Bye."

"Why do I feel like my brother's hiding something?"

"Or someone?" We both laughed.

"Seriously though, I hope he's okay."

So do I.

19

LOURDE

"This is so much better than the other store." Olivia's eyes widened as she took in the rack of evening gowns.

"And here you're telling me you didn't want to spend much." I chuckled, eyeing up the backless midnight blue dress and thinking how much Barrett would love it.

"Well, I may have lied there." She laughed, picking up a dress off the rack. "Oh, look at this one!"

"Ms. Diamond, how nice to see you again."

"Hi, Patricia," I said, smiling at the owner of the design shop I frequented over the years.

"Is it that time of year again?" she asked.

"Yes, it is, and I have a special guest who needs to shine for all the bachelors in the crowd."

"This is my dear friend and boss, Olivia."

"Hello, and no, I'm definitely not your boss. But, dear friend, I'll take, though." She winked.

"Lovely to meet you. Well, let's see, you are tall with beautiful hips, so let's see if I can pull some suggestions for you to try, so we can get them fitted in time for this weekend."

"Great!" Olivia squeaked out, and I don't think I'd ever seen her get so excited.

While Olivia was in and out of the changing room, I took a moment to check in on Pepper, asking how she was doing. When my phone pinged, I assumed it was her but was pleasantly surprised.

Barrett: *Where's my dollface at?*

Lourde: *We took the afternoon off. Olivia and I are dress shopping for the ball.*

Barrett: *Well, well, are you trying to get in trouble again?*

I bit my lip, remembering how he had filled me… *everywhere.*

Lourde: *Sorry, boss, was I not supposed to?*

Barrett: *Definitely not. Hurry home. I'll charge the batteries.*

"Ha." I let out a chuckle, blushing at the thought. I looked up to find Patricia taking me in, a smile crossing her perfectly made-up face.

"Okay, how's this one?"

I put my phone down as Olivia pushed the velvet curtain aside and walked out in a chiffon and tulle baby blue gown.

"You look like Elsa standing in her ice castle," I shrieked, taking in the blue explosion of color.

"And you look like the cat that swallowed the canary." She popped an accusatory eyebrow, then her gaze fell to the extension of my arm where my phone lay face down.

I laughed. "It's nothing."

"And by nothing, you mean Barrett. But yeah, I'm not digging it either," she said. "Okay, next."

An hour later, Olivia had picked *the* gown, and it suited her to a tee—a teal green halter neck dress with a teasing hint of cleavage. Of course, it was the Diamond

Charity Ball, after all. There was certain etiquette to follow.

"Thanks for today," Olivia said, hopping out of the car Barrett sent to pick us up.

"It was fun."

"Nice to see your face has gone back to normal. Maybe next time you're sexting with the boss, do it away from me. Ugh!"

She shut the door and let out a grin.

"I don't know what you're talking about."

"Uh-huh. Sure you don't. Go, enjoy. Say hi to him for me," she said, turning toward her apartment.

"Tribeca or Mr. Black's home, Ms. Diamond."

"Mr. Black's please, Jimmy."

"Of course."

Over the last week, I'd left more and more things at Barrett's. What started with an extra toothbrush had turned into a drawer of clothes, and a few articles of clothing hanging in the 'hers' part of his walk-in closet.

He insisted,and I had to agree. It made sense. I spent way more time here than I did in Tribeca.

* * *

His hand fell around my throat as he sunk into me. Feeling fullness everywhere, I fanned my fingers out on his sheets, gripping the fabric, and my skin tingled.

"You like being naughty, don't you, dollface?"

"Yes." I dragged in a shallow breath. Then, curling my hand around, I cupped his balls in my hands, lightly squeezing. A deep husky groan reverberated from his chest as he continued to give it to me from behind, faster and deeper.

I gasped, feeling the dildo slide inside my back hole,

bringing me to the brink, then back down again as he continued with his malicious mischief.

Consumed by the heavenly fullness, I curled my fingers as heat bloomed inside my chest.

"Now you can come, Lourde," he commanded. His gravelly voice was my undoing, and I dropped my head, submitting to his command and unraveling in waves around him.

"Fuck," his dick quivered inside me, shooting his load as his hand fell around my hips. He lowered his head, his lips showering my skin with gentle kisses.

20

BARRETT

My phone pierced the silence. *What time was it?* It was still pitch black, and Lourde was beside me asleep.

Quickly, I felt for my phone on the nightstand and silenced the ringer while I got up and walked outside my bedroom. Ivy's name flashed on my phone.

Why the fuck was my media director calling me?

Closing the door behind me, I put the phone to my ear. "Ivy, what's going on?"

"I'm sorry to call you at four in the morning, but this couldn't wait."

The edge of her tone caught me off guard, and an unsettling feeling nestled in the pit of my stomach.

"What is it?"

"Jessica, who we thought had disappeared, well, she's back, and she released a statement about you."

"About me? What about me? I hardly knew her."

"Not according to her. She alleges you assaulted her."

"She fucking what?"

My neck ticked with a rage I had only reserved for my father. "That is complete and utter nonsense. What the fuck?"

"I'm sorry to tell you this, Barrett. The papers are running the story in the morning press. It will be syndicated nationally."

Fuck, Lourde. The bottom of my stomach lurched. *What would she think?*

"Barrett, are you there?"

"I'm here."

"They want a comment from you."

"I'll give them a fucking comment. I didn't do it!" I yelled down the phone.

"Unfortunately, with the allegations out there, it doesn't matter if you did or you didn't. She's smeared your name, and it will be tarnished for good."

"I know."

"But you didn't do it, right? Actually, scrap that. I'm obviously deliriously tired."

"Of course, I didn't fucking do it, Ivy! I would never assault anyone."

"I know. I don't know why I asked that. Anyone who works for you can attest to you never crossing that boundary. You're always so professional with the staff."

I took my hand to my head, realization settling in as my chest constricted. "Why is she after me like this? First the fire at 21 Park, then the crane accident, and now this. Someone wants to bring me down, and I'm going to fucking stop it. *Now,*" I yelled.

"What do you want me to do?"

"Round up the team. Wake up everyone… Jesse and Barton from security and anyone else you can think of and meet me in the office in twenty minutes. I want my lawyers to sue her ass. We're putting a stop to this bullshit now before it ends up costing me everything."

I hung up the phone and threw it across the floor, smashing it into little bits of twisted metal across the concrete.

"What's wrong?" Lourdes' meek voice shook me from my fit of rage. I turned to find her in a camisole and shorts in the hallway, regarding me with concern.

Fuck, how could I tell her this? How could it tell her I'd let her down? I'd let her family down and, most of all, let myself down by not finding out who was fucking me over before things got truly out of hand.

"What is it?" she asked, walking over to me.

I put my hands in my hair. "Something's happened."

"What, is your sister okay?"

"Evelyn's fine. I've had a serious allegation leveled at me, and it's making the news today."

"What is it?"

I sat down, not able to look her in the hazel eyes. She sat next to me, putting her hands in mine. I don't deserve her. *I fucking don't deserve her.*

"Jessica, who effectively you replaced in Olivia's department, is accusing me of sexually assaulting her."

She gasped, and I looked up to find her eyes wide like saucepans.

"It's not true, obviously."

"Of course, it's not true."

I breathed easier, knowing she believed me without even having to convince her.

"What did you think? I thought it would be true?"

I shrugged. "I don't know."

She shook her head. "Well, you obviously don't know how much I love you if you think I'd doubt you."

A scowl fell across her face.

"Sorry, I just didn't know what anyone would think, let alone the one person I love and care about the most."

She squeezed my hand. "Okay, well, how are we going to tackle this?"

"We?"

"Yes. I'm with you all the way. That's if you want me to be?"

"Of course, I do. But this doesn't look good on you, Lourde, and your family."

"I'm with you," she repeated.

"Okay, let's talk about it later. I have to get changed and go into the office to meet everyone."

"I'm coming with you."

"No." My voice came out more forceful than it should have, and I instantly regretted my tone.

She looked at me, hurt.

"I'm sorry, Lourde, I got myself into this mess, and I have to do this on my own. I'll call you later."

I walked away, leaving her with a painful expression plastered across her beautiful face. I just couldn't bear to see her that way?

* * *

After three hours of meetings, I felt like we were going in circles. Sure, we'd taken the necessary legal steps to sue her for defamation. We'd also drafted an official response my lawyer was set to read to the press, but we weren't any closer to finding out the *why*. Like why Jessica, who I hardly knew, would want to hurt me like this? What her motivation was and if there was a connection to whoever it was after me.

But that was it. We were no closer to finding out the why.

Despite my team's best efforts, we were no closer to finding out who was behind the crane incident or the fire.

Maybe this was my penance for what happened to Mom. Fuck, I pushed the nonsensical thought away.

Olivia poked her head through the boardroom. "Got a minute?" she asked, pulling me out of my downward spiral.

"Yes. Guys, can you give us a moment, please?"

"Perfect, I'm starved," Ivy said.

"Food should be out there. I asked Aimee to arrange it on my way in."

"Thanks, Barrett," they all looked at me like I'd given them a lifeline.

"Olivia, come in."

A low hush came over the room as everyone exited. The weight of the press had hit the building in a shroud of bullets, shattering the work culture I'd built up in an instant.

"Close the door."

"You sure that's a good idea after the recent allegations."

"Jesus, fuck, Olivia."

"Okay, sorry, I had to lighten the mood somehow."

I laughed. God knows how under the circumstances.

She sat down. "I know this isn't true. Everyone who knows you knows this isn't true. You have hundreds of testimonies in this building alone."

"Thanks, Olivia."

"I don't get it."

"I don't either, but someone's out to ruin me."

"Are you any closer to finding out?"

"They say we are, but I don't know."

"How's Lourde with it all?"

I looked up at her, my heart heavy, my shoulders slumped forward.

"Oh," she let out.

"No, she's fine. She's supportive as hell."

"Then what's the problem?"

"I've missed three calls from her brother and four from Alfred."

"Alfred Diamond?"

"They can only call for one thing."

"And I'm guessing that's not to check in on how you are."

I shook my head from side to side. "Absolutely not," I breathed out in an icy whisper.

"Surely, they know this is all fabricated. It's nonsensical."

"It doesn't matter if it's not true. The Diamonds live and die by their reputation."

"No, you don't think…"

"I know. I don't have to think."

"Jesus, Barrett, what are you going to do?"

"I'm going to return their fucking calls. That's all I can do."

"I'm here if you need me, okay?"

"Thanks, Olivia. Actually, there is one thing I need."

She got up. "What's that?"

"I need you to take Lourde offsite today, anywhere, take her to the sites at Soho or Greenwich. I can't have her here with all this going on."

A perplexed look crossed her face. "Are you sure?"

I glared at her.

She threw her hands up in the air. "Okay. Okay. She will not like it, but okay."

"I wouldn't normally ask you to interfere, but today, I'm under extraordinary pressure."

"I get it. But this is the first and last time I get in the middle."

"I know."

She nodded and turned her back, walking out of the boardroom.

I turned to my new phone. The missed calls were adding up—Magnus, Ari, and my sister had called a bunch of times. Then all the texts and messages of support from business associates came flooding in.

But it was the missed calls from the Diamonds that were burning a hole in my chest.

I turned over my phone and dialed up the last missed call to Alfred. It only rang once, and he picked up.

"Barrett, I know you're busy, so I won't keep you. Come to the house tonight with Lourde at six sharp."

"Okay," I said, and there was a pause before the line went dead.

There was no use pretending what tonight was about, and he didn't sugarcoat it.

I fired a text off to Lourde.

Barrett: *Tonight… your parents at six.*

Three dots immediately flashed on the phone

Lourde: *I know. Why are you ignoring me? Can we go together?*

Barrett: *I'm sorry, busy. I'll meet you there.*

Not wanting to be around her for fear of hurting her more, I thought it was best.

Lourde: *Love you x*

. . .

I began typing the same words back that had become so natural to say, but something stopped me, and I put the phone face down.

"You're all right to continue?" Ivy stuck her head through the doorframe.

"Yes, come in," I said, ignoring the dull ache in my heart.

21

LOURDE

With Olivia to my left, we watched Jessica's live interview unfold on my phone outside ZF's Soho boutique hotel. I felt sick to my stomach as she spooned out lie after lie, force-feeding it to anyone who would listen.

TV Anchor: *"Tell America what happened that fateful night, Jessica."*

Jessica: *"It all started when he asked me to work late for a meeting. I thought it was going to be my design manager and me, but it was just him and I, in his office alone. He moved alongside me, and the next thing I knew, his hand was on my thigh, rubbing it suggestively. It was then I knew I was there for another reason."*

TV Anchor: *"And what reason was that?"*

Jessica: *"He said he could advance my career if I got on my knees."*

TV Anchor: *"So let me get this straight. ZF Construction's owner and multimillionaire tycoon, Barrett Black, invited you to his office under the pretense of work when, in fact, he was inviting you to perform fellatio in exchange for a promotion?"*

. . .

"What absolute bullshit," Olivia spat out in a fit of rage.

I just stared at the screen, unable to form the words in my mouth. Instead, time seemed to slow down as a heaviness formed in my stomach.

Jessica: *"Yes, exactly."*

TV Anchor: *"And what happened next?"*

Jessica: *"I pushed his hand away and got up to leave."*

TV Anchor: *"Then what happened?"*

Jessica: *"As I was opening the door to his office to flee, he yelled, don't come back."*

TV Anchor: *"So, did you file a case for unlawful termination?"*

Jessica: *"I have my lawyers working on that now."*

TV Anchor: *"Well, thank you for speaking out, Jessica. We have invited Mr. Black to come on the show to tell his side of events, but we haven't received a response to that request. His team, however, has vehemently denied any accusations you have leveled at him."*

Jessica: *"Typical."*

Pepper and Grace had called when it was question time and checked in to see how I was doing, which was fine because I really couldn't listen to any more of her lies and betrayal. I was fucking livid. Mad to the core that someone could lie blatantly on live television and ruin a man's reputation just like that. Destroy everything he'd ever worked for in one minute of airtime.

"Shh, quiet down," Pepper said. "I just heard your name, Lourde."

Grace and I went silent, putting a lid on my rage for the minute.

TV Anchor: *"What do I think his girlfriend, Lourde*

Diamond, would make of your accusations?" she said, repeating the question.

Jessica: *"I guess I hope she just sees him the way I do and protects herself."*

"Fuck you!" I screamed out. This cannot be happening to us.

"That fucking bitch," Pepper said.

"I can't believe this, Lourde," Grace added.

I felt Olivia's hand across my shoulders, but it was doing little to calm my fireball of nerves. I needed to call Barrett, and I needed to get the hell out of this development and go to him.

"Girls, I have to go. I have to see if he is okay."

"Call me later," Pepper said.

"Take care of yourself," Grace added.

I inched the cell over so Olivia was in the screenshot. "Olivia's got my back."

"I do," Olivia added and waved at the girls on the screen. Unfortunately, it was their first introduction, not how I wanted them to meet.

"Thanks, Olivia," they both said in unison.

As soon as I heard my name, I knew I was a target. And Olivia read my mind when she'd ushered me to the nearby car and directed our driver to take me home. She'd offered to stay, but I sent her away. I needed to think. I needed to understand how I could help Barrett.

All afternoon I paced my apartment, hoping to find some clarity to the messy situation we were in. At the bare minimum, to help Barrett. But mad as a rattlesnake, I still couldn't make sense of it all.

It didn't help that my calls to Barrett went unanswered. All five calls, to be exact. And when I was getting ready to go to my parents, I was so goddamn desperate to speak to him, I called Aimee, his assistant, and pleaded for her to put me through to him.

After holding on the line for what seemed like forever, it was her voice on the other end, not his, relaying a message from Barrett that he'd meet me at the Diamonds as planned.

Okay, fine, he was busy. Whatever, but it was me. Supporting him was at the top of my list, but I couldn't do that if he wasn't letting me in. His guard was up, and it was time I tore it down completely.

By nightfall, there was a media pack waiting out front of my Tribeca apartment. Luckily, Pepper had cleverly created a decoy so I could slip out undetected out the back. We'd done it a few times in the past, fooling the photographers when we hadn't wanted to be snapped, and it had the desired effect.

Dad had messaged me earlier, stating the obvious— *don't talk to the paparazzi*. But I was two steps ahead of him. If I could handle anyone, it was the paparazzi. Born and raised into the Diamond family kind of prepares you for life in the public eye.

But Barrett was private, always had been. never making a fuss or calling media conferences. Even when his prestigious hotels and towers opened, he always had others speak at the opening.

He wasn't afraid. Barrett wasn't scared of anything. He was just incredibly private, and with his upbringing, it all made sense why. Why draw unnecessary attention to yourself when you could cruise through life undetected while building an empire?

He was the opposite of my family. The Diamonds waved their money and notoriety around like it was oxygen, hosting parties, charity balls, attending benefits, and every social event in the calendar. Mom lived in the tabloids, dragging Dad along with her, and she loved every moment.

* * *

There was a serious undertone disguised as a polite greeting in the room when I entered. *What had I interrupted?* Were Dad and Connor at it again, or was this about Barrett and me?

Mom, Dad, and Conner were all seated around the dining table. Barrett hadn't arrived yet. With an empty plate and half-finished drink in front of him, I wondered how long Connor had been here.

"Darling. How are you doing?" Dad remained seated as I came round to kiss him on the cheek.

"I'm okay, I guess. I just feel for Barrett."

"Yes, it must be difficult for him," Mom added.

After greeting Mom and Connor, I sat down next to the empty chair. A terrible feeling settled at the base of my stomach.

I hadn't eaten all day—that must be it.

I picked at the cold meats and cheeses, trying to make the feeling go away. "Have you spoken to Barrett?" I asked Connor.

"No. He hasn't taken my calls, but I imagine he's been in crisis talks all day."

I nodded. *Yes, that's why he hasn't called you back, Lourde.*

"Anyway, why did you call us both here? Do you have a plan that can help Barrett?"

I looked up to find three sets of eyes on me.

"Lourde, we—"

"Good evening," Barrett said, cutting off Dad.

Dressed in the same suit had he rushed out the door in

this morning, tiredness plagued his handsome face. His eyes met mine briefly, his mouth flattening into a strained smile.

I stood up to greet him, the legs of the chair scratching along the floorboards. I pressed my lips to his, but all I got in return was a peck before he turned to greet the others.

Swallowing down the thickness that lined my throat, I took my seat at the table, nervous about what was about to unfold.

22

BARRETT

She pulled back and took me in. I barely kissed her back and with none of the same intensity we normally shared. I'd ignored her calls all day. I couldn't face the embarrassment I'd caused her—the humiliation I had brought upon her perfect family name. But typical Lourde, she just wanted to be there for me, and I pushed her away.

It didn't matter what Jessica said was utter bullshit. My name was smeared. They had syndicated her report throughout North America, and my company was in disarray. Sure, that fucking bugged me, but I was a phoenix. I'd risen from the ashes before, and I could do it again and again.

Any day now, my team was going to uncover who was behind this clusterfuck, but that didn't matter right now. My name was mud, and anyone associated with me had been dragged into this mess too. That brings us to here and now, and I wondered if Lourde had any idea why we were here because I sure as fuck knew.

I just didn't know if I could go through with it. I think death would be worse than what was coming.

"Should we sit?" I offered.

She looked at me warily. "Can we talk?" she whispered.

I looked down at her and smiled, knowing it would put her at ease. "Later, okay?"

"Barrett, thanks for coming," Alfred said. "We know you are busy, so we will keep it brief."

"Are you hungry?" Elizabeth asked.

"No," I said, wanting to get this over and done with.

"How you doing, bud?" Connor asked. I hadn't taken his calls either, nor Magnus and Ari's calls.

"Been better."

"Unfortunately, we are here under terrible circumstances," Alfred offered. "I know you have the best team around you, but I would like to offer you our support. If there is anything you need from us, we are here for you."

I looked at him. What?

"Privately," Elizabeth added. "We are here for you privately."

Connor shook his head.

"What's going on?" Lourde looked at her brother, then Elizabeth.

"Lourde, you can't see Barrett anymore," Alfred said.

"What are you talking about?" She almost laughed at the ludicrousy of it. Perhaps she had no idea it was coming.

Fuck.

Connor turned to me. "And Barrett, you're a smart guy. You would have seen this coming," he said, his tone serious.

I nodded. I saw it coming all right. As soon as that bitch Jessica opened her mouth and ruined my own happily ever after.

"Barrett?" Lourde turned to face me. Her wavering voice shot me in the chest.

I stared back but couldn't form any words for a response. Sadness changed to anger as Lourde averted her gaze to her parents. "This is bullshit."

"Lourde, language." Elizabeth looked down at her nails, then took a deep, loud inhalation, catching everyone's attention. "Lourde, you know as well as anyone, our name is like a religion, held in the highest regard since Grandpa Alfie built the empire. You must know there is no way I can associate us with this mess," Elizabeth said.

"Well, I don't care. I love Barrett. He loves me. We stand by each other in times of crisis."

"No darling, I'm sorry. We forbid it."

"I'm twenty-three years old. You can't forbid it!" She got up and screamed at them. "Barrett, come on."

I remained seated with Alfred staring at me. His eyes held a warning behind them I fully understood. But I just couldn't do it to her. I didn't have the courage. I needed her more than anything. Slowly, I quietly stood.

"Barrett, do what's right." Connor's voice held a warning.

I ignored him and went to her. Her face was plastered in anger and hurt, her eyes glossy, threatening to spill over with unshed tears.

* * *

On the quick trip back to her apartment, she fidgeted nonstop, irate with her family for calling us over to the ambush. I let her vent. Saying otherwise was like standing in front of a Mack truck, so I let her talk to calm down.

When we pulled up to the back entrance of her apartment, the paparazzi had it covered.

Fuck.

"Don't say a word," she said.

I killed the engine, opened my door, then went around to open Lourde's. In a matter of seconds, they surrounded us. Flashing bulbs, pushing and shoving, and a barrage of fucked-up questions were thrown our way.

"Barrett, is what Jessica said the truth?"

"Do you regret that night?"

"Lourde, why are you standing by him?"

A vein ticked in my neck, and I wanted to punch every one of them out with an iron glove.

She squeezed my hand as if sensing my rage, and I shielded her from the crowd of people gathered around.

"You can do so much better than a monster, Lourde."

Suddenly, her hand pulled out of mine, her body torn away out of my protection.

No!

"Stop!" Lourde yelled, reaching for me, the fear in her eyes casting a chill up my spine.

Pushing aside whoever was in my way, I reached for her hand, yanking her back into the safety of my arms. We'd reached the gate, and when I looked over my shoulder, the same fucker who grabbed her before was trying it again, this time throwing me a sly smile as he was grabbing her arm.

That was it.

With Lourde's back against the gate and me standing in their way, I shoved my hands on his chest, pushing him back with a raging force—Jessica's press conference, The Diamond ambush, and his prick of a smile in one thunderous push that leveled him to the ground.

"Shit," Lourde cried behind me.

He landed on the pavement, his head hitting the sidewalk. Cameras punched and bulbs flashed in strobes of bright white.

He gripped the side of his head. "You're going to pay for that, Barrett."

Sue me.

I didn't give a fuck. I just wanted to get her to safety. A moment later, we were inside, riding the private elevator to her floor. The click of shutters and yelling voices had faded away to soft elevator music.

"Are you okay?" I scaled her from head to toe, unsure what I was looking for.

"Yes, I think so." Glancing down at her clothes, someone had ripped her blouse in the colossal fuck of getting from the car to here. "That was crazy," she said.

"They will do anything to get a headline, even provoke me, like that cocky little fuck."

"Barrett, now you'll be up for assault charges."

"He attacked you, Lourde. I don't give a fuck."

"I know," she whispered.

Fear clouded her eyes as she remembered the incident. I replayed the scene in my head as the elevator ascended. The doors pinged open, and I stood glued to the floor, reality punching me in the guts with a full-body punch.

I knew what I had to do.

I trudged behind her into her living room, like walking through wet cement.

Heavy legs.

Heavy heart.

I had to protect her. I couldn't protect my sister or my mother from my violent father, but I could protect Lourde.

She threw her arms around me, her body against mine. Her tongue pushed past my teeth as I opened for her, matching her intensity in one last kiss. With the adrenaline of the crowd and everything I had, I kissed her back. I pulled her so close, wanting to taste her, breathe her in.

Then I pulled away quickly.

"Why did that feel different?" she asked.

I sighed. "Because your family's right, Lourde."

"No, don't say that," she said.

"With these allegations leveled against me, it paints you in a bad light."

"We can get through it. Together."

My heart ached. There wasn't any way around it. I could see it now.

"No, it's too complicated. I'm too complicated." I stepped away from her, not trusting myself this close to her.

"Okay, I'll admit this situation isn't easy, but—"

"But you deserve someone from a good family, Lourde, from an uncomplicated past."

"Like Finigan?" she huffed out.

Just hearing his name on her lips made me fucking mad as a rattlesnake. He was everything I wasn't.

"He is from a solid family."

What are you doing, Barrett?

It pained me to say it, but it was true.

She put her hand on her hip. "So you don't love me anymore, is that it?"

I love you like a drug.

When I didn't answer, her face fell to the floor.

Looking back up, her eyes spilled over with tears. "You coward! I thought we were it… you… me."

I did too. I really did.

"I'm sorry, Lourde."

"Go. Get out!" she yelled.

"Lourde, please…" I reached out for her, but she stepped away.

"I'm a fool. I am a goddamn fool for ever wanting you, Barrett. You're the worst thing that's ever happened to me."

Her eyes widened with hate, reaching for the counter to steady herself as her hand trembled.

She'd delivered the knockout punch, and I was down for the count. I didn't care about my company or my reputation. I just let the one thing that mattered most in my life go—and all because I loved her.

"I know. I always told you I'm an asshole. Goodbye, Lourde."

A stake pierced my heart, and I was bleeding out. That's what it felt like when I rode down the elevator and away from love.

23

LOURDE

I t had been days since we'd broken up, but whoever said time heals all wounds must have meant more than a few days because this wound was fleshy and raw as hell. Feeling sorry for myself and crying my lungs out in despair, I hadn't left my apartment since Monday when I asked him to leave. How Barrett could do this to me was unfathomable. To make things worse, he wanted to push me onto Finigan. *Finigan!*

Weeks ago, when he was forced to endure Finigan and me flirting at dinner, he couldn't stand it. But now? Barrett, along with Mom, Dad, and Connor were teaming up to push me onto him.

I wasn't a violent person, but I felt like throwing and smashing everything in my way. I hated my parents for what they had done to us. Even more, I hated Barrett for not being the man I thought he was and stepping up at the very moment I needed him to.

Giving up on us was the easy way out, and he grabbed it with both hands. Maybe I was better off without the drama. Maybe he was too much work. Childhood trauma can do that to a person, molding them in a way where you gave up on relationships at the first hint of trouble. I buried my head in my hands, letting the salty tears flow.

I felt vibrations against my foot, and I wiped the tears away. My phone rang on the floor—again. I let out a sigh, then waited for it to ring out before deciding to pick it up and check the multitude of messages I'd been ignoring for days. Eight missed calls from Pepper and now a text popped onto the screen.

Pepper: *If you don't let us up, I'll make a scene so big it will make Kim Kardashian's sex tape look like a confession.*

Shit. They were here.

All week, I'd been ignoring their calls, and now they were out front with the paparazzi too. Still camped out for some kind of exclusive—they hadn't left since the scandal broke.

The metal tone of the buzzer sounded, reminding me of their presence downstairs, and I let out a groan.

I didn't want any visitors. Not even my best friends. Maybe they'd just give up and retreat if I didn't answer.

My phone buzzed again. I turned it over to find a message from Olivia.

Olivia: *Pepper is here about to address the media. This friend of yours is ruthless—I like her. You have ten seconds…*

Double shit.

Pepper *would* do something. She loved the limelight. I groaned again, then folded off the lounge, dragging my heavy legs to the intercom.

Pressing the button, I readied myself for whatever was coming. I glanced around my apartment, throwing my hands in the air, not even trying to attempt the mass cleanup that was so desperately needed.

I caught sight of myself in the mirror and ran my

hands through my brown hair, trying to smooth down the frizz from days of neglect.

Again, what was the goddamn point?

Maybe turning away my housekeeper wasn't a smart move. Looking around now, clothes, magazines, and half-eaten takeout containers littered the space. Glassware had stacked up near the sink, and I'm sure the apartment needed airing out. As I breathed in, a concoction of left-over sushi and rancid red wine filled my nostrils.

The elevator pinged, and the doors opened. Olivia, Pepper, and Grace stepped out like the Charlie's Angels trio, looking immaculate and making me realize how out of touch I'd been with society. I looked down at my sweats and soy sauce-stained t-shirt.

Yeah, okay, so maybe a change of clothes was in order. I looked back up, and three sets of eyes regarded me.

"Jesus, Lourde. When you told me you and Barrett had broken up, I didn't think you would ignore me for the rest of the week and go into a cave!" Pepper shuddered visibly at the sight of me. Stepping in, she pulled me close, giving me a bear hug.

I gripped her back, finding comfort in familiarity. After a minute, I let go.

"When's the last time you showered?" Grace asked as she kissed me on the cheek.

"I can't be sure," I said, smelling my clothes and letting out a laugh. The sound was foreign to me. Actually, moving was entirely foreign to me. I had slept on the couch most of the week, only getting up to use the toilet and answer the door for food delivery.

"How are you holding up?" Olivia asked, coming over and wrapping her arms around me.

"Look at this place!" Grace squeaked out.

"Sit down if you can find a spot. I'm fine, though.

Really, you ought to just go home."

"We aren't going anywhere." Grace moved some empty containers off the chair and onto the coffee table, then perched precariously on my armchair.

I sat back down on the couch with Olivia as I watched Pepper get busy cleaning up the dishes and kitchen area. "You're lucky rodents didn't overrun this place," she said, picking up something with a finger pinch grip.

"How is he?" I asked Olivia, unable to hide my feelings for the man who broke my heart.

"I don't know. You know how private he is. But he's not the same. He's definitely not the same without you. He's keeping busy with all of this media stuff going on."

"Are they any closer to finding out who set him up?"

"I think so. Listen, how are you doing?" Olivia asked, taking in my disheveled appearance then placing her hand on my knee.

I flopped back on the lounge. *Now there's a question.*

"Lourde, hun, talk to us," Grace added.

"I'm angry. Angry and confused."

"What happened?" Olivia asked.

"Isn't it obvious?" Pepper said, turning around from the kitchen. I was surprised she was even in there cleaning up—Pepper and domestic duties were like Superman to kryptonite.

"Her family put an end to the relationship. The Diamond name is too important to be embroiled in a scandal like this."

"God, you sound like them," I said.

She blinked, then returned to cleaning up the mess. "Well, I'm right, aren't I?"

"But surely they can see past the lies? Couldn't you and Barrett just tell them it was all lies?" Olivia asked.

"It doesn't work like that," Grace said, shaking her

head at Olivia.

"Are you all the same with your upbringings?" she asked.

"Yes," Grace and Pepper said in unison.

"Our families came from old money, so they know that reputation in this city is a currency on its own," Grace added.

"And she's not saying that to be snobby either. It's just the way it is when you reach a certain level of wealth."

"Is that true?" Olivia turned to me.

"Afraid so. But I'm sick and tired of putting my family above my happiness."

"It's just the way it is, Lourde," Pepper said.

"But my own brother, he knows how much Barrett and I mean to each other, he could have defended me, but he just sat there."

"Maybe he didn't know what to say?" Pepper shrugged. The way she always came to his defense was downright irritating now.

"That's bullshit."

"Look, your mother contacted me to check in on you," Pepper said, changing the subject.

"She wants to remind you the ball is tomorrow night."

"Fuck the goddamn ball!"

"You have to go. You're making me go!" Olivia said.

"And as much as I just met these girls and love them already, I want you there, Lourde."

"Actually, how did you guys get in touch?" I asked, ignoring their pending question.

"Do you know how easy it is to slide into someone's DMs?" Pepper inquired.

"It's true. There aren't many Peppers that slide into my DMs, mainly just horny guys," Olivia said.

"I can be a horny guy," Pepper said in a husky baritone

voice that made us all spill over in laughter.

"Ah, no thanks," Olivia said.

"So we're all here to see if you're okay and to get you out of a funk because that is what best friends do."

"And what better way to do it than to get you all dolled up into a new ball gown?"

"Grace?" Olivia said.

Grace got up and moved over to the elevator, where a rectangular box was.

I hadn't even noticed it when they'd walked in.

"This is for you," Olivia said as Grace popped it on my lap.

Okay, so maybe for the first time, my mood had changed from somber as fuck to moderately happy.

"Open it." Pepper hovered around.

I opened the lid off the box, and staring back at me was a navy-blue dress. It was backless too. *Wait.* "Is this the dress I tried on with you, Olivia?"

She nodded, a huge grin on her face. "It is."

I lifted it out of the box and stood to admire it. "How did you do this?"

"I asked the designer for a favor. She had your measurements from previous dresses."

"Why?" I asked.

"Because you loved it, and you were too busy helping me get the perfect dress, you forgot about yourself."

"Never forget about you, Lourde," Olivia said.

"Thank you." I put the dress down and hugged her.

"Hey, how about us too?" Grace asked.

"Sorry," I said, wiping a tear away. "I'm so lucky to have you all in my life," I said, pulling away from Grace to hug Pepper, who gave me a brief hug.

"So, does that mean you're coming?" she asked.

"I guess it does now, you sneaky bitches!"

24

BARRETT

I was a frigging destroyer. I was on the warpath, and if I wasn't happy, then fuck, why should anyone else be. My staff was in the firing line of my flippant and often erratic behavior. But I didn't give two fucks—I couldn't stop.

We were inching closer to finding out who framed me, and bothering to come to work was harder than my dick around Lourde. Not because of the shitstorm that had fallen upon us this week from Jessica's barrage of lies. No, not that. Rather because of the shell of a heart in my chest since Lourde and I were no longer together.

But it was my fault. I pushed her away when I should have leaned into her. It was a necessary evil, and there was no turning back now. If I hadn't, I'd be ruining her future along her family's reputation and legacy.

But when I returned home to an empty house, reality struck like barbwire to the heart. She was gone, and I was gut-wrenchingly hollow. The darkness had eclipsed my heart, and again I lived in the shadows, licking my wounds in my own private Idaho.

"Barrett, sorry to trouble you, but I have something important." Barton stuck his head through the door. My goddamn assistant must have let him in when I strictly said no one was to come in.

"Fuck, it better be good. I asked Aimee to leave me the fuck alone."

"I know." He closed the door behind him. "But listen, I found out who's behind this, and you won't believe it."

"Get in here then," I snapped.

"Yes, of course." He leaped over and sat on the chair opposite me. "The camera that picked up the face cutting the wire near the crane we identified as James Crowset."

"Never heard of him."

"No. Nor should you."

"Can you get to the point?"

"We connected him to the Hamptons' board members, Simon and Cary.

"Do you have proof?"

"It's all in there." He slid an envelope toward me.

Opening it, I quickly scanned the first photo. The fucking lump in my throat rose to my tongue. Pictures of him cutting the crane cable were there, but I'd seen those. Behind them were covert pictures showing the board members and him in a room together.

"This isn't enough. It's good, but not enough."

"I knew you'd say that, so I dug further, finding a money trail of small regular payments to James from a trust fund."

"Let me guess who the directors of the shady trust are."

"Both board members."

Fucking cocksuckers. I knew they were snakes, but I never knew they had this in them."

"Good work."

"Thank you, sir."

"When you met them in the Hamptons a few weeks back to negotiate the purchase of the iconic Hamptons Hotel, did you have any idea then?"

"They didn't like that I lowballed the fuck out of them and accused them of skimming the hotel of hundreds of thousands of dollars to fund their mistresses and holidays... if that's what you mean."

"Right. Well, fuck. They are behind it, pure and simple."

"And how does Jessica's declaration of lies tie into all of this?"

"They recruited her. First of all, to give access to the worksite, so they knew when the security detail switched, then to come up with the absurd lie accusing you of sexual harassment."

"I don't understand why she'd do it... I barely knew her."

"What other reason is there?"

"Money."

Of course.

"We traced a lump sum to an offshore account that links back to a Jessica Anne Wiles."

"How much?"

"Two-hundred thousand."

"Fucking cheapskates."

"Yeah." Barton snorted out a laugh.

"You know better than anyone, Barton. I reward loyalty. Under Olivia's leadership, she would have excelled and earned that in a bonus alone."

"I know how generous you are, Barrett. You'll find everything in the dossier in front of you."

"Have you informed anyone else of your findings?"

"Not yet. We came to you first. Jesse Frisello and me, that's it."

"Good."

He eyed me. "You don't seem overly happy at the finding."

Why would I be? I lost her. I lost everything.

"I'm thrilled," I said, feigning a smile.

"O… kay."

"Go. Have some time off. I know you and Jesse have been working nonstop on this."

"Thanks, Barrett," he said, getting up to leave.

"Oh, and Barton… good work as always."

"Thank you, sir."

* * *

I sat on the discovery, and when I got home, I poured myself five fingers of whiskey and then some, drinking until I passed out cold.

A bang in the living room startled me, and I quickly shot up, which I really shouldn't have because my head thumped like a herd of predators. I looked over to the side of my bed. The bottle of whiskey was half empty.

Fuck, that would explain it.

Another clatter in the kitchen.

Who was here? Please tell me I didn't call a fuck for the night. Bile rose in my throat. *Fuck, no.*

I flung the sheet off me. Thank fuck I wasn't naked. I still had yesterday's clothes on. I walked over to the door, trying to hear any signs of who may be on the other side of the wall.

What if it was Lourde who was here? What would I say? I don't know if I had the strength to push her away again.

Don't be ridiculous. The look in her eyes when I pushed her away was a pain worse than death. *She never wants to see you again.*

My heart sank. If it wasn't her, then…

"Fuck." A throbbing pain hit my chin bone, shooting past my knee cap.

What the hell!

A chair had been placed near the doorframe. *What the fuck was that doing there?*

"Barrett, is that you?"

"Evelyn?" I rounded the corner and walked from my bedroom.

"It's me!" She walked over to me, and the first thing I noticed was her walking had improved tremendously. Round-the-clock therapy since her last operation was working.

"Holy shit, look at you!" I said, pulling her in for a massive hug. She held me and hugged me back. It was a hug I desperately needed, and damn, I'd missed my sister.

"You smell like a pub!" she said.

"Thanks, sis. What are you doing here?"

She threw the tea towel over her shoulder and rolled her eyes.

"You called me."

"I did?" I don't remember. Shit, if I called her, who else had I called?

"You called me at nine o'clock last night not being able to string two words together."

I rubbed my forehead. "I remember little about last night."

"Well, you're lucky because I was already on my way to see you when you called."

"Why did you leave Boston?"

"Because you hadn't called me back all week. I'd tried so many times, and I was so worried about you."

"You didn't have to come, Eve," I said, sitting down at the kitchen counter.

"Ah… yes, I did."

"No, you didn't," I reiterated.

"Stop being all macho around me, Barrett. Take my support. You've always taken care of me. Now it is my turn to take care of you." She handed me two Tylenol and a glass of orange juice. "Here, take this," she said.

"Thanks," I said, gulping it down.

She looked at me. "You look like shit."

"That's support?" I asked, wide-eyed, and laughed.

"Well, support can come in different ways." She grinned. "Are you hungry?"

"Oh, hell no," I said, the contents of last night's whiskey churning in my stomach.

"You need a nice fat greasy burger."

"Oh God, don't even…" I held my churning stomach.

"By the look of you, I bet you haven't had a burger in years."

"You're right, there."

She sat on the stool next to me. "So tell me why did this skank Jessica make up these lies about you?"

"Ha, well, that's a story."

"Wait, let me make a coffee first. I'm exhausted from watching you in the chair last night."

"That's why there's a chair in my room?"

"Someone needed to make sure you didn't choke on your own vomit."

"Oh God, sorry."

Over the next hour, I filled my sister in on everything. Starting with the fire at 21 Park which was arson, to the cut crane cable, and Jessica's press conference of lies. All of these events were traced back to the three board members of the Hamptons Hotel I'd just bought because I found out they skimmed two million off their hotel and laid off employees to cover their asses. I engineered a cut-throat deal. One where they lost.

"I can't believe someone would go to these lengths to destroy you."

"Oh well, they did."

"Why haven't you exposed them? You said you've got proof of the money trails. They can go to jail for what they've done."

"I found out last night."

"And?"

"And then I got hopelessly drunk."

"Because?" She narrowed her eyes. "Should you be happy about this... oh."

"I don't care about any of it anymore if I don't have Lourde."

"Why isn't she standing by you?"

"She wanted to."

"Let me guess. You pushed her away."

I raked a hand through my messed-up hair. "I didn't have a choice, Evelyn."

"You always have a choice, Barrett. You're the one who told me that, and it's always stuck with me."

"Not with this. Her family said we couldn't be together."

"But it was all lies! Anyone could watch that press conference and see straight through her lies. I wanted to slap her across the face and shake the truth out of her when I saw that."

"It doesn't matter, Evelyn. None of it matters. The Diamonds are royalty in America. They couldn't have their daughter, heir to their fortune, associated with someone with sexual assault allegations leveled at him."

"And what are you, chopped liver? You have built an empire, Barrett. Your name means something too."

"Not anymore."

"Well, fix it. Clear your name. You have the documents that implicate them and show the world Jessica is a lying bitch." She slammed her fists on the countertop, a few drops of her coffee spilling out.

"Calm down."

"I don't understand how you're not screaming to the rooftop about this. You have the proof."

"I will, trust me. I will take them down like the pieces of shit they are, but it stops nothing between Lourde and me. It doesn't fix a goddamn thing." I pushed my seat out and walked off.

"Barrett, wait."

"Just leave me, Evelyn, please," I said and walked off to my bedroom. My headache fucking aching.

* * *

It was the afternoon by the time I resurfaced. Speaking with my media manager and detectives, I'd spent the entire morning strategizing, and it was about to play out in front of my very eyes.

Holed up in my home office all morning, we'd run a faultless plan that saw both Hamptons' directors already arrested. What I had installed for Jessica was much more than an arrest—it was a public apology. She needed to repair the damage and do it in the same public way she ruined my reputation in the first place. Truth was, I couldn't give a fuck about my name anymore. My empire could crumble around me for all I cared—although my staff, I didn't want them to suffer. But everything meant nothing without *her* in my life.

I walked outside to find Evelyn relaxing in the living room with the television volume turned all the way up.

"Well, someone's been busy." She averted her gaze from me back to the large screen on the wall, where I tuned into the news anchor on screen.

"*Breaking news: Arrest made following fraud and defamation, news press to follow shortly.*"

"Evelyn, I guess I should apologize for walking off before. I just have a lot going on, which I know is no reason to be huffy at you, but you know…"

She patted the space on the couch next to her, and I sat down. She lowered the volume on the remote.

"I know, but sometimes you need a little push if you veer off course, and I think you may have with Lourde."

"I can't do anything about it. I've just got to accept that this is it. Her mother is probably arranging her marriage to Finigan Connelly at tonight's charity ball."

"Finigan Connolly, the governor's son?"

"Yes, he comes from old money and a long line of politicians… perfect husband material for Lourde."

She laughed. "Ah, I don't think so."

"What do you mean?"

"Finigan Connolly makes Charlie Sheen look like an angel."

"What are you talking about? The guy's reputation is cleaner than my asshole."

"Please don't mention your asshole around me again, and no, I guarantee you it's most certainly not."

"Well, go on!"

"Think black book of prostitutes and endless prescription drugs on tap."

"You're pulling my chain." I laughed.

"Not at all."

"There's nothing in the press."

"Of course not. They own all of Boston. They just pay off whoever they need to, to make these stories disappear."

"And you know this, how?"

"My physiotherapist's sister, who is a doctor now, worked the scene for a while."

I raised my eyebrows. "Worked the scene?"

"Don't judge, Barrett. She had to save money for her college tuition. Being a doctor doesn't come cheap, you know. "

I gestured impatiently, needing her to continue.

"Anyway, dear old saint Finigan was one of her clients."

"No shit."

She nodded.

"And this hasn't made the news?"

"Politicians are protected. Apparently, she signed a non-disclosure agreement as long as her arm... her and a bunch of his regulars had to do the same."

"Lourde has no idea. I bet you her mother's already booked the venue."

"Well, I guess you should go to the ball then?"

"I can't go to the ball. I'm not invited. Anyway, could you imagine if I showed my face at the annual Diamond Charity Ball? Alfred and Elizabeth would murder me. Not to mention what Connor would do if he found me there."

"Don't jump to conclusions. Look at what's on the news right now. They'd see this, Barrett. This news is huge!" She pointed at the screen, and we both turned. Footage of the board members being arrested flashed on the screen.

"With this, your name is cleared," she exclaimed.

"Not yet. Jessica needs to make a public apology in exchange for her freedom."

"How did you manage that?"

"It's what I do, sis. The thing with Jessica is she really wasn't to blame. She was a pawn in their game to ruin me. It turns out she needed the money for her sick sister's treatment in California. She was so apologetic, crying on the phone to my media director."

"Since when do you offer anyone leeway? The Barrett I know would have fed her to the wolves."

"Maybe I would have in the past, but nothing comes out of that. I'd just be ruining her life when all she did was make a serious error in judgment."

"Lourde's softened your edges." She scratched her head. I guess it was out of character for me to spare someone. "So now what?" she asked.

"Jessica will be live on television within the hour with her statement of apology. I don't have to hear it. I know what she's going to say. So, it's just back to business for me, just like it never happened." I exhaled, my lungs heavy with unshed air. "I just go on like I always have."

"And forget about the love of your life? I see the way you talk about her. Your face comes alive and lights up, and before shutting back down again, you do the same whenever we talk of Mom."

"You can't blame yourself for any of this, Barrett. I bet you still blame yourself for Mom, don't you?"

"Maybe, I don't know. There will always be something there, some element where I let not only you down but her too."

"You haven't let me down at all, Barrett. You've helped me every day, paying for my surgeries, physio, and a roof over my head."

I shook my head. "You know what I mean, Eve."

"You tried saving us from him! He was the monster. If it weren't for you, I'd be dead. Stop blaming yourself for Mom. This guilt is stealing your life away from underneath your very eyes. You need to quit giving up so easily when it comes to your happiness because you deserve every happiness this life has to give you, and if that happiness comes from Lourde Diamond, you've got to fight for her. Fight for her tonight at the charity ball. Show her how much you love her and how sorry you are for giving up on love. And guess what?"

I stared up at her.

"I'm going with you."

25

LOURDE

I watched Jessica's teary apology live on the screen with my family around me in my parents' den.

"Now, can you see?" I asked, turning to Dad. His serious look didn't give too much away, nor did Connor's.

"Mom?" Her mouth pursed into a thin line, but apart from that, nothing. Injectables had frozen any emotion as she sat there in her beautiful makeup, ready for the ball.

"Well, sorry, sis." Connor walked up to me and slapped me on the back.

Okay, well, that's a first, but I'll take it from my brother.

"It doesn't change a thing." Mom stood up, smoothing down the satin dressing robe.

Dad glared at her but remained silent.

I muttered out a sound I couldn't recognize. "What do you mean, it doesn't change a thing? Barrett is in the clear in the public eye. You got what you wanted! This proves none of this was his fault!" This time, it was my time to stand, squaring off with my mother, seeing my father didn't have the gall to do it.

A phone's melodic tone sliced the tension.

"I've got to take this," Connor said, grabbing his phone. I waited uncomfortably for her to answer me back.

"His reputation is mud, Lourde."

"No, it's not! He's cleared."

"It's already been tarnished. There's no coming back from that."

"You can't be serious?" I turned to my father, dressed in his bowtie and black suit. "Dad, please?" I begged.

Dad looked up, then back down again after Mom turned to stare him down.

"Let's just enjoy tonight's ball, and we can discuss it tomorrow," he said, offering me a weak smile.

"Do my feelings get a vote here?"

"Feelings? What do they have to do with anything?" Mom scoffed at her own comment.

My chest burned with rage. "I love him with everything I am," I spat out.

"He pushed you away. He broke it off, Lourde. At least he had the decency to do that."

The pain stung as the words left her mouth.

Would he take me back?

Would he ever forgive me for my family's actions?

"You left him no choice."

"There's always a choice, dear, and he chose not to be with you."

My throat clogged with emotion, her words poison ivy.

"Elizabeth, that is too harsh," Dad said.

"Since when do you care about feelings, Alfred? You especially don't care about embarrassing me, do you?"

"Don't bring us into this. This is about our daughter."

"Besides, Finigan is perfect for her. He will be at the Plaza along with two hundred guests very soon, so for once, I agree with your father. Let's talk about this tomorrow. Not on the most important social day of the year."

"Finigan and I will never, ever happen, Mom, get it through your head."

"He is perfect, Lourde!" she reiterated.

"If he's so perfect, why don't you marry him!" I yelled. "Whatever's going on between you two, obviously isn't working!"

"Lourde!" Mom gasped, her face blooming with color.

"Well, she's right, isn't she, Liz?" Dad said, his revelation flooring me. *What is going on with the two of them?*

She blinked erratically. "I'm not... this is... not what I'm doing right now," she stammered. "I have makeup waiting."

"And there you go again, ignoring reality when it smacks you right in the face."

"No, Alfred!" She raised her finger to Dad and walked away, pausing to look over her shoulder. "Lourde, I'm sorry, it's just the way it is." She turned back around and headed out the door into her quarters.

Tears pricked the backs of my eyes, but they dare not spill.

I felt Dad's hand on my shoulders, pulling me in for a hug. "What's going on with you and Mom, Dad."

"It's what's always been going on, Lourde. You're just more aware of it now. Or maybe I'm too old to hide the cracks of our marriage. But this isn't about your mother and me."

He turned toward me. "Do you love him, Lourde?"

I looked up at dad. "Yes."

"Okay."

"Okay?" I asked. "What does that mean?"

"It means leave it to me to fix."

"But Mom?"

"Forget your mother," he said, nudging me.

I sighed. "Dad, this is something I have to fix."

"Really?" he questioned in surprise.

"Truly. But as long as I know you have my back, I might be able to repair the damage I've caused."

"You can count on me. My little girl is all grown up and fighting her own battles."

"That's what we do as Diamonds."

"Sure is. Now come on, let's enjoy the ball. You always have."

"Thanks, Dad," I said, watching him leave the room.

I flopped back down on the couch. The revelation of Jessica's speech, the arrests of the Hamptons' board members, and Mom wanting to set me up with Finigan. It was a lot to digest.

But the truth surrounded my heart like a warm blanket. The truth had not changed. My feelings for Barrett had not changed. I still loved him. Painfully so.

But did he still love me?

There was only one way to find out.

* * *

"What are you doing on your phone again?" Pepper asked, glammed up in a red sweetheart cupped dress, her black curls down her shoulders.

"He's not calling me back," I said, staring down at my phone at the unanswered calls. Okay, maybe I looked like a stalker at this point, but I really didn't care. Since the press conference, I'd lost count of how many calls I'd put through to Barrett.

Then there was the stark reality he was happy without me.

"Look up and around. It's such a beautiful night," Grace said, pulling Dane's arm closer to hers.

"I am," I sighed, but I was slowly losing hope that

Barrett would call me back. I don't know why I had any in the first place after what my family did to him.

"Sometimes men need to come to their own conclusions, Lourde," Olivia said, holding my hand before Ari once again cornered her into a conversation.

Since arriving yesterday, Olivia and the girls had been my rocks. And seeing Olivia in her beautiful dress seamlessly fitting into our friendship circle was the icing to a crummy situation.

Mom had strategically positioned Finigan at our table in place of Barrett, but I hadn't said two words to him all night. Getting the hint, he'd left soon after entrees, cozying up with barbie lookalike herself, Ariya Crestwood, the daughter of the sugarcane king of America, Marty Crestwood—which was fine by me.

Connor returned, taking his seat next to Magnus. "God, do you think just once, Dad's board could stop talking to me?"

"Has Alfred set a date yet on announcing his retirement?" Magnus asked.

"If he has, he hasn't told me. But that means nothing. He doesn't tell me much."

"Just try to enjoy tonight," Pepper said across the table, and all eyes set on her.

"What? We all should. It's the annual ball. Why let anything affect you? Same goes for you, Lourde."

"Yes, it's certainly not the same without Barrett here, is it?" Connor stated, sighing.

"He's been a fixture like the caviar table for years at the ball," Ari added, coming up for air after chewing Olivia's ear off.

"I know he donates a fortune, too," Magnus added.

"I don't care how much he donates. I don't want him here for his money," I said through clenched teeth.

"I know, sis. Of course, I know that." Connor threw me a kind smile. "Look, auction time is about to start. Maybe Pepper is right. Let's just try to enjoy the rest of the night. After all, tonight is all we have. There is no guarantee for tomorrow."

"I'm not going to be up there with you tonight, Connor. I just can't."

"Mom will have a fit, Lourde. Are you sure?"

"I don't care."

"Fair enough. Well, I still need someone to help me out up there."

He stared at Pepper and shrugged. "Want to be my sidekick?" Connor raised his eyebrows.

"Are you sure?" Pepper looked from Connor to me, and I shrugged.

"Why not?"

"Okay! Thanks, Lourde!" She shot up, and heat bloomed up her neck.

Was it me, or was there something going on there? Could Pepper be the reason my brother was in such a good mood lately? No. I shook my head. He wouldn't, not after he grilled me with shacking up with his best friend. Plus, Connor was a player, and he didn't deviate from blondes.

* * *

The auction was coming to a close, and Connor was the best MC to ever live. The crowd loved him, the microphone an extension of his arm as he entertained and swooned the crowd. He and Pepper were dynamite up there, raising way more money than ever before.

But I kept staring down at my phone. If I needed a clearer message that Barrett wasn't interested, it would be the lack of response.

I pushed my chair out as sadness washed over me. I couldn't be here anymore. I'd done my part and just needed to be alone.

"I'll see you later, Olivia. I have to get out of here," I whispered in her ear.

"Wait, where are you going?" she asked, pulling my arm down.

"He doesn't love me. He doesn't want me. I need to get out of here." I pulled away from her before I gave the crowd the satisfaction of spilled tears and another headline.

26

BARRETT

My heart thrashed about like a bull in a cage. Evelyn's hand fell on my forearm as though sensing my discomfort. She looked beautiful in a pale pink floor-length gown hand-picked for her by my stylist, who rushed over at my last-minute request.

I watched from the back of the room. Round tables with gold overlays, gold centerpieces, and the warm glow of festoon lights hung overhead in the grand ballroom. She'd had a year to plan this event, and Elizabeth had thought of everything down to the custom his-and-hers fragrances. Just with the guest list alone, the paparazzi would cream their panties, which would be talked about for months to come.

All eyes were on Pepper and Connor as they ran through the list of auction items until they were at the last item for the evening.

"So that concludes tonight's auction items," Connor said, and my heart instantly took flight, landing in the middle of my throat.

Right on cue, Alfred walked up on stage, whispering into his son's ear as the audience grew quiet.

Connor turned to his father, his eyes widening to the size of golf balls.

"Ladies and Gentlemen, it appears that wasn't the last item up for auction. We have another last-minute item for auction. This item is not in the catalog and is a first for the Diamond charity. Men, get ready to sell some blue-chips for this one as I'm sure it will be the most expensive item we've ever had."

Oohs and aahs echoed around the room, but my gaze settled on Lourde. Dressed in a stunning navy satin dress with loose waves falling around her mid-back, I hadn't been able to take my eyes off her since arriving.

"Okay, Okay. Settle down. Jimmy, can we go to the live item?" Conner asked.

If I thought my heart rate had spiked, now it was off the charts.

The large screens on either side of the stage changed from an image of the Diamond logo to a ring.

Women in the audience chatted animatedly, no doubt trying to convince their husbands or partners to bid. Bid away, people.

Connor read from the piece of paper his father passed to him.

"The last auction item for the evening is a ten-carat emerald cut flawless diamond. Wow. You heard correct, ten-carat flawless diamond!"

Gasps erupted from the crowd.

"Flawless and impeccably designed, this…" he went on for what felt like fifteen minutes. All I could hear was my heart in my ear pounding as blood passed through it. Evelyn held onto my arm, not letting go.

"Do I hear an opening bid or offer?"

"Three hundred thousand dollars." A man near the front popped up his white paddle to signify his bid.

I laughed alongside a few others who knew the true value of such a priceless item.

"Mr. Percival, really?" Obviously, Connor was one of them. "We all like a bargain, but that's a steal!"

"Okay, half a million." He laughed. "It was worth a shot."

"Thank you, Mr. Percival. We have half a million dollars. Do I have any other offers? This is truly a master-piece handcrafted."

"Six hundred thousand." A gruff voice cut through the silence.

The spotlight shone where the sound came from in the middle of the room.

Decent bid.

"Excellent bid, sir. Can you hold up your paddle, please?"

"Thank you, the bids with you, number thirty-one."

My gaze fell to the table where Lourde was standing behind her seat, looking as though she was about to walk away.

No.

The two of them were going back and forth, and the price had crept over the million-dollar mark.

I didn't have time to wait any longer with the battle of the cheapskates. It was now or never. And never was not a possibility when it came to Lourde.

"Two million dollars," I said, my voice boomed from the back of the room.

Heads turned, and gasps were louder than ever when they realized where it came from.

But I was only interested in one person, and she turned around immediately after hearing my voice.

Her hazel eyes hit mine.

I moved out from the shadows, the spotlight finding me and lighting me up.

"Barrett?"

I ignored the voices and began to slowly walk toward her. Everything around me fell away, the shrieking noises, the warm ambient lights, the smells of the expensively prepared banquet. It was just her and me and none of the prying eyes.

I knew I'd taken a gamble, and it could backfire, but it was one I had no choice but to take. Fight to the death or fall hard. We were about to find out which.

"Do I hear any other offers? No? I didn't think so."

"Going, going… sold to my dear friend, Barrett Black."

Eventually, I arrived at her table as applause billowed and echoed around us. She stood in front of her chair, her arms trembling as they held on to it for support.

"You came," she said, her breath hitched as I paused a hair's breadth away from her.

"I got your messages," I said, breathless myself.

"What, I mean…" She looked down then back up again.

I stepped in closer to her, my mouth grazing her ear, and she shivered at the contact.

"Lourde, I was a fool for pushing you away."

"Yes, you were," she said, but there was a kindness to her tone.

"I hope you can forgive me."

"Forgive you? I'm sorry I let my parents interfere. If you'll have me back, I promise that will never happen again."

"Oh, I know it won't." Curiosity swept across her face. I smiled, wanting to put her at ease.

She gripped the chair tighter. "Barrett, you just bought a ring." She sucked in a large influx of breath.

I stepped back just enough and bent down on one knee.

"Oh, my God, what are you doing?" She held her hands to her mouth as the audience shrieked around us.

"Lourde, I know I'm a complicated man, and you could have anyone, but I love you so much, I can't breathe without you. I will be the husband you need me to be every damn day in this life together... so please, Lourde Diamond, will you choose me?"

27

LOURDE

He looked up at me with his green eyes, sincere as his pure heart. This extremely private man had made the most public of gestures and was down on one knee before me and hundreds of others. And he wanted me to pick him. I'd picked him forever. It had always been him.

He knocked on the door to my heart five years ago when he drove me home from my debutante ball. Then he captured my heart in the Hamptons, where he never left.

"Dollface? I could really do with a yes right now." My gaze focused on Barrett, and his eyes widened as I realized he was still staring at me for an answer.

I took an intake of breath. "I choose you, Barrett. It has always been you."

The audience broke out into a raucous of claps and cheers. The cheers of Olivia, Ari, Grace, and Dane echoed behind us.

He got up, and the next thing I knew, my feet were off the floor, his arms around me as he buried his lips on mine.

I threw my hands around his neck and groaned into his kiss.

"You had me worried," he said, resting his forehead on mine. "And nothing worries me."

"Someone has to keep you on your toes."

"You like to be naughty, don't you, dollface?"

"Only for you." I let out a breath, and my lips fell on his in a tangled kiss—a kiss that marked the beginning of our story.

"Hey, you two, come over here!" Olivia's voice cut through our embrace, and we pulled our lips off one another to the hugs and cheers of our close friends— Olivia, Ari, Grace, and Magnus.

"We were holding our breaths for a while there!" Olivia said as I made my way round to Barrett's side.

I felt Barrett's had slid into mine as we hovered around the table holding champagnes the waiter had handed to us.

"Tell me about it, he said, squeezing my hand, and I squeezed it back.

"I think I was just in shock," I said.

"You're not the only one in shock." Connor appeared with Pepper by his side, fresh from their auctioneer duties, surprise etched on his face. He wrapped his hands around me and squeezed me in for a hug. I let go of Barrett's hand to welcome his warm embrace.

"Oh my God!" Pepper squealed and joined in the hug, wrapping me up in a Pepper and Connor sandwich. "We have so much to plan!" she said, pulling away.

"I can't wait!" I shrieked.

"I wonder if Mom and Alfred will be off my back now you're engaged," Connor stared vacantly. Betrothed to Francesca, the daughter of Duke and Duchess Cavendish, Connor's arranged marriage was to be announced when Dad stepped down from Diamond Incorporated.

"Ha, doubtful. Where is Francesca anyway? I saw the two of you talking before at her parents' table."

"Who knows." Connor laughed nervously, taking in Pepper then me.

Did I miss something? Before I could register, Connor stepped forward and shook Barrett's hand. "Well, Barrett, you pulled a fast one over all of us!"

"It wasn't intentional," Barrett said as Connor followed through on the handshake with a man hug.

"How did you do it?" Connor asked, and my ears pricked up.

"I'm curious too. How did you get Dad to go along with this?"

"You don't need to know everything, Lourde." Dad appeared with Mom trailing behind him.

"Alfred." Barrett smiled as Dad pulled him in for a hug. "Thank you."

"No need to thank me, son, I know you'd do anything for my Lourde. You can't hide true love. Dad said, beaming with pride as he slapped Barrett between the shoulders.

Wow. How on earth did he win Dad over?

"Now, where's my little girl?" I stepped into Dad's embrace. "Darling, you've made me so proud."

"Thanks, Dad." I kissed him on the cheek.

"Congratulations, dear." Mom kissed me carefully, making sure not to ruin her makeup. She then did the same with Barrett standing beside me. She stood back and stared at both of us. Trying to make sense of the last ten minutes, a flash of confusion appeared on her beautiful face but was quickly replaced with her Oscar-winning smile the minute her friends surrounded her.

"I'll catch up with you two love birds later," she said as a friend pulled her away. She looked back and smiled at me. A smile lit up her eyes. There was no denying his massive gesture won her over, plus every other woman in the room.

"I best mingle too, darling," Dad said, kissing me on the forehead.

"Dad, wait." I held his hand, stopping him from leaving. "I don't know what Barrett said to you to make you change your mind about us, but I just wanted to say from the bottom of my heart, thank you."

"You deserve to be happy, Lourde, and I know Barrett is the only man that has your heart. You have to hold onto love, it's a rare thing." He winked, then disappeared into the crowd.

I turned to find Barrett talking to someone with similar features to his—soft green eyes, dark hair, and olive skin. She was stunning. He guided her as she walked solely toward me, a cane in her hand.

Evelyn.

"Lourde, I'd like you to meet someone very special to me."

"Evelyn," I blurted out and pulled her in for a hug. She squeezed me tight and after a moment, I released her.

"Well, aren't you a beauty! No wonder my brother is completely obsessed with you."

"It goes both ways. I'm completely obsessed with him too," I said, and he stared at me then his sister.

"I'm the happiest man in the world right now."

Evelyn pecked him on the cheek. "You deserve every bit of that happiness, brother." She looked at him for a minute, then her gaze shifted to mine. I noticed her eyes were glassy.

"… and Lourde, we are going to be sisters!"

I shrieked out excitement as we embraced again. Barrett introduced Evelyn to our table of friends, and Evelyn took a seat next to Magnus and Ari. The waiters topped off all our glasses full of champagne, then Connor cheered us.

Back slaps and cheering swirled around us as the girls started brainstorming the perfect wedding venue. Greeted with eye rolls from the boys, they quickly changed the subject to wedding cars which went on for I don't know how long.

"How about the honeymoon?" Pepper's question cut through the back and forth.

"Bora Bora is meant to be beautiful," Olivia exclaimed.

"More like how about the bachelor night," Magnus added with back slaps from Connor and Ari.

Barrett leaned in, his mouth on my ear. "Come with me," he said, his gravelly voice low. Exhilaration shot up my spine as his breath set off the familiar ache between my thighs.

He stood, then held out my chair. "Wait, where are you two going?" Pepper asked.

"Just taking my fiancé for a spin on the dance floor," Barrett said.

"But we were just going to talk about the wedding dress," Grace stressed.

"I'm sure you guys have it covered." I smiled, unable to quell my excitement about being alone with Barrett. The wedding dress could be a fucking rainbow at this point.

He squeezed my hand, and we both slid away from the table toward the dance floor. Abruptly, he took a sharp left, so we were heading back behind the band and through a black velvet curtain.

The band's road cases were the only thing back here,

and we were surrounded by darkness, the idle chatter of the guests nearby barely audible.

He spun me around, his warm breath on my skin. "I can't wait any longer to have you."

"Well, don't," I whispered.

His lips crashed onto mine as our tongues desperately claimed one another. I held the lapels of his jacket and pulled him into my chest. He groaned in my mouth, then lifted me onto a road case pushing my legs apart and standing between my thighs. I felt his thickness through the satin of my dress, and an ache throbbed between my legs.

He left my mouth and went on his knees, pushing aside my lacy thong, his tongue dipping into my folds. I gripped his hair in my hands and moaned at his burning touch.

"Fuck, I love you, dollface," he said before burying his face between my legs.

"I love you," I said, tilting his face up to meet mine. "Barrett, I need you inside me, now." The desperation threatened to take over my entire body.

He stood, and I quickly made light of his belt, button, and zipper, freeing his engorging erection.

He clasped my face in his hands and kissed me deeply as he entered me. With my butt at the edge of the road case, he held me in place, entering me further. I wrapped my hands around his neck, absorbing all he had to give me. A throaty groan left his lips as he buried himself inside me, deeper and deeper.

Heat coursed through my body in a delicious burn, and as I came, I bit down on his jacket, stifling my own moans.

"Lourde," he moaned as he shot his seed into me.

His lips ravaged mine in a kiss that was breathy and warm, sending my body tingling with emotion.

After a minute, we disentangled.

"And to think, we have our whole life to do that again

and again," Barrett said, unable to wipe the smirk off his face.

"Mr. Black, don't tempt me for round two," I teased.

He grinned. "We should get back before they notice we're missing."

"Could you imagine Mom's face if someone caught us back here!"

He stopped me from walking ahead. "Wait, Lourde. There's one more thing."

Reaching into his jacket pocket, Barrett produced the heart-stopping flawless diamond ring.

"Our forever starts tonight, dollface," he said, holding open the ring box.

I gasped. "Barrett, it's stunning."

He slid the ring on my finger, then traced my fingers with kisses. Turning my hand over, his lower teeth grazed my palm, sending a flutter to my core. "Now, back to that round two…" His eyes flared.

I kissed him on the lips, pulling him close. "You're on."

EPILOGUE
CONNOR

I watched my sister return with Barrett from the dance floor. I was so happy for them. Truly. The whirlwind of events that had shaped tonight had me on the edge of my seat.

When Alfred whispered an engagement ring was next up on the auction card, it threw me completely. But Alfred does that. That's Dad. I'd stopped calling him Dad early on when he looked at me with an odd expression I'd never forgotten.

But tonight wasn't about me as much as my parents wanted me to butter-up Francesca for our impending nuptials. Tonight was about Lourde and Barrett. And as I watched his hand caress her forearm and her wrapped in his arms, I couldn't be happier for her. She'd gone through so much with men, and I was partly to blame.

Together with Mom, we tried to arrange suitable men for her to date. After all, we expected her to marry a partner from a similar background and one who could be mutually beneficial to both families. That's how it was done in the past.

My parents had my suitor lined up a long time ago, and it was nearly time for me to wed. Cue the beautiful Francesca. I cast my eyes toward her table. Long and leggy with perfect silicone tits, Francesca was stunning. We got along too, casually fucking from time to time. But tonight, when Francesca wanted to fuck, I rejected her, putting myself and the Diamond family in a precarious position.

This week, Pepper was in my bed, her black curls, olive skin, and curves had me begging for more, and I didn't beg. I wanted to take her back to my place again and hear her scream my name in waves of orgasm after orgasm.

I wanted to forget all responsibility.

I wanted to push away my father.

I needed to sink myself inside of her.

But that wasn't the reality, and the secret, casual encounters we'd had, had to stop. Alfred was likely weeks away from retirement, and the billion-dollar empire would fall squarely on my shoulders. And if I wasn't careful, I could fuck it all up. Generations of wealth and reputation gone in an instant.

I couldn't be doing this. Like the countless women before her, Pepper was just an escape. If it wasn't her, it was alcohol. And I'd certainly been abusing that recently.

I sighed just as Lourde's focus settled on me. I smiled back, putting her at ease. She worried too much about me. Sometimes I wish it was Alfred who worried, but that was a wish that fucked off into the wind years earlier.

"You all good?" she asked loud enough over the table so I could hear. Magnus was busy talking with Evelyn, Barrett's sister, while Ari had taken to Olivia—a stunning, take-no-shit blonde. But next to me, Pepper sat quietly, falling in and out of conversations around me. I wondered for a moment if she saw Francesca drape her arms around me earlier.

"He's probably just tired, right, Connor?" Barrett said.

"That's exactly it. Think I need to sleep for a week."

I watched Pepper excuse herself from the table. Her hips swayed with each step she took, and the fabric of her dress clung to the curves of her ass as she walked toward the ladies' room. My dick twinged in response.

With everyone engrossed in conversation, I pushed out my chair, knowing exactly where I wanted to go.

Walking across the dance floor, I stopped outside the bathroom and leaned up against the wall. A moment later, Pepper stepped out, and I grabbed her hand, pulling her around the corner and away from prying eyes. I pressed her back against the wall and pushed my groin into her silky thighs.

"Connor, what if someone sees us?" she murmured.

"I don't give a fuck," I said, slamming my lips against hers in a heated kiss.

She groaned and dragged her tongue inside my mouth, wrapping her arms around my neck and pulling me close. After a bit, it took all my energy to pull away. *Fuck.* I was this close to fucking her against the wall at my family's annual ball.

"Here, take this," I handed her the swipe card. "The penthouse. One hour."

She ran her gaze over me suggestively, then took the card and tucked it into her purse. I stepped back, giving her space to peel herself off the wall.

"Now go." I slapped her on the ass.

"Connor Diamond, behave." She walked ahead, tossing me a wink over her shoulder.

"Fuck, no."

. . .

I waited until Pepper had returned to take my seat. The same discussions flowed around the table, and I was confident no one even noticed we were gone.

I pulled my chair underneath the table and closer to Pepper. Discreetly, I ran my hand down like I was tying my shoelace, but instead, my hand slid up the inside of her thigh.

I heard her gasp when my hand reached her upper thigh.

"This is just a prelude," I said in a low voice as I ran my hand up and down her folds through her lace underwear. *She was* soaking *wet for me.*

Francesca approached the table, stopping just behind Lourde, and only a few feet from me.

Pepper stilled, but I didn't care she was here. My fingers massaged her clit, pulling a gasp covered with a cough from her lips.

"Congratulations, Lourde. Barrett." She removed her penetrating gaze from me and returned it to Lourde and Barrett.

"Francesca, thank you!" Lourde gushed, standing to embrace her.

Pepper lowered her hand underneath the table in an attempt to swat my hand away.

But when I didn't budge, she quickly gave up.

"Connor, till next week." Francesca smiled seductively.

"Looking forward to it," I said, driving my hand harder against Pepper's clit.

Francesca remained, hanging back. She likely wanted me to escort her back to her table. When she realized I wasn't moving, the tips of her ears turned pink, and she huffed out in annoyance, turning and walking away a moment later.

"She is one foxy woman." Magnus tilted his head, following Francesca disappearing into the crowd.

"Magnus, you can't say that about his fiancé," Ari said.

Pepper tensed again at Ari's words.

"She's not my fiancé," I said in a stern voice.

"Yet," Ari added.

Cocksucker.

Angry, I subtly quickened my pace, rubbing my fingers in a circular motion against her clit. Pepper gripped the champagne flute as I felt her ever so subtly begin to tremble. Her legs squeezed my hand, locking it in place for the briefest of moments before relaxing.

I released my hand and used it to adjust myself under the tablecloth as Pepper gathered her composure.

"Connor, that was rude," Lourde said, taking the bait like I knew she would.

"Your right, sis, that was pretty rude. I should probably say goodbye to Francesca," I said, excusing myself from the table.

"Enjoy your goodnight *kiss*." Magnus grinned.

"Might get more than a kiss," I said, tossing Magnus a wink. Both Olivia and Evelyn shook their heads in mock disgust.

"Connor, gross!" Lourde let out in a groan, and the table erupted into laughter.

Francesca was the perfect ruse. And now I had the perfect reason to escape.

I lowered my mouth to Pepper's ear.

"Penthouse now."

ALSO BY MISSY WALKER

SLATER SIBLINGS SERIES

Hungry Heart

Chained Heart

Iron Heart

ELITE MEN OF MANHATTAN SERIES

Forbidden Lust*

Forbidden Love*

Lost Love

Missing Love

Guarded Love

SMALL TOWN DESIRES SERIES

Trusting the Rockstar

Trusting the Ex

Trusting the Player

Forbidden Lust/Love are a duet and to be read in order. All other books are stand alones.

JOIN MISSY'S CLUB

Hear about exclusive book releases, teasers, discounts and book bundles before anyone else.

Sign up to Missy's newsletter here:
www.authormissywalker.com

Become part of Missy's New Private Facebook Group where we chat all things books, releases and of course fun giveaways!

https://www.facebook.com/groups/
missywalkersbookbabes

ACKNOWLEDGMENTS

To all my new fans who found me via Tiktok! I never knew such a powerful platform existed for indie authors such as me.

Boy was I wrong.

The booktok community is super huge and super cool and I've made so many new friends and fans by sharing my fav book scenes and snippets.

You guys are truly amazing!

Cheers,

Missy x

ABOUT THE AUTHOR

Missy is an Australian author who writes kissing books with equal parts angst and steam. Stories about billionaires, forbidden romance, and second chances roll around in her mind probably more than they ought to.

When she's not writing, she's taking care of her two daughters and doting husband and conjuring up her next saucy plot.

Inspired by the acreage she lives on, Missy regularly distracts herself by visiting her orchard, baking naughty but delicious foods, and socialising with her girl squad.

Then there's her overweight cat—Charlie, chickens, and border collie dog—Benji if she needed another excuse to pass the time.

If you like Missy Walker's books, consider leaving a review and following her here:

instagram.com/missywalkerauthor
facebook.com/AuthorMissyWalker
tiktok.com/@authormissywalker
amazon.com.au/Missy-Walker
bookbub.com/profile/missy-walker